The Ties That Bind

The Ties That Bind

Electa Rome Parks

New American Library

New American Library
Published by New American Library, a division of
Penguin Group (USA) Inc., 375 Hudson Street, New York, New York 10014, U.S.A.
Penguin Group (Canada), 10 Alcorn Avenue, Toronto,
Ontario M4V 3B2, Canada (a division of Pearson Penguin Canada Inc.)
Penguin Books Ltd., 80 Strand, London WC2R 0RL, England
Penguin Ireland, 25 St. Stephen's Green, Dublin 2,
Ireland (a division of Penguin Books Ltd.)
Penguin Group (Australia), 250 Camberwell Road, Camberwell, Victoria 3124,
Australia (a division of Pearson Australia Group Pty. Ltd.)
Penguin Books India Pvt. Ltd., 11 Community Centre, Panchsheel Park,
New Delhi - 110 017, India
Penguin Group (NZ), Cnr Airborne and Rosedale Roads, Albany,
Auckland 1310, New Zealand (a division of Pearson New Zealand Ltd.)
Penguin Books (South Africa) (Pty.) Ltd., 24 Sturdee Avenue,
Rosebank, Johannesburg 2196, South Africa

Penguin Books Ltd, Registered Offices: 80 Strand, London WC2R 0RL, England

Published by New American Library, a division of Penguin Group (USA) Inc. Originally
published by Xlibris Corporation.

First New American Library Printing, October 2004

ISBN 0-7394-4708-4

Set in Bembo with Chalet
Designed by Daniel Lagin

Printed in the United States of America

Not a day goes by that I don't think of you. Not a day . . . You left me too soon; I wasn't ready to let you go. A part of my heart was buried with you on that cold, wintery day. I remember your laughter, your smile, your courage, your words of encouragement and wisdom as if it were only yesterday. Mostly, I remember your love. Even though you're gone, I feel your spirit shining down on me each and every day—my guardian angel.

As a gentle breeze caresses my cheek and the sun shines upon my face, I feel your presence and know that you are proud.

This is dedicated to my mom, affectionately known as Dot, who we lost on January 29, 1997, to breast cancer. You are missed, never forgotten, and forever loved.

Acknowledgments

Foremost, I would like to show my appreciation to the Lord Jesus Christ for this moment, for this opportunity, for my life, and the gift to tell a great story. God is good!

To my husband, Nelson, thank you for believing that I had a story to tell and an audience that wanted to read it. Thank you for believing in me every time I failed to believe in myself.

To my children, Brandon and Briana, you have shown me the true meaning of love, life, and family. I'm so proud of you.

To my sister, Tresseler Rome, thank you for your encouragement, your friendship, for reading, reading, and rereading my manuscript and for just being you. "Yeah, whatever" (smile).

To Laymon Taylor, thank you for showing me that to be a dad, you don't have to be the birth father. Thanks for making me feel loved now and always.

To my nephew, DaJuan Crooms, keep being a cool little boy who grows into a strong, black man. And Jordan, I love you, too.

Sharron Nuckles, what can I say? You are an original. Seriously, thanks for being in my corner. Thanks for the encouragement, the support, the friendship. Thanks for the late-night critique sessions, the phone calls, and the editing. I am forever grateful to have you in my life and honored to have you as a friend.

To my family members Catherine Dorsey, Carolyn Rome, Audrey Thomas, Effie Stroud, Avorn Stroud, Buffie Stroud, Pamela James, Dexter James, Alvin Rome, Beverly Rome, my assortment of cousins, thank you for showing me the true meaning of family.

Heather Franklin Flippin, thanks for being a part of my life.

Thanks for the love and support you radiate each time I talk to you.

Betty Rakestraw, thank you for being a play grandmother to my children and for being like a second mom to me. It means so much.

Patricia Crimes, thanks for saying "You can do it" and for believing in my dream. Thanks for listening to my crazy stories at work when we should have been working. Tell Sally hello and don't forget to pick up your packages. Call me, lady!

To Marzella Marley, Katrinda Porter, Shunda Blocker, and Andrea Parnell, thanks for the initial feedback you provided. It was invaluable.

Kimberla Lawson Roby, Timmothy McCann, Hope. C. Clarke, Maggie Breaux and Tim Everett, thanks so much for the feedback and answering my many questions.

A huge thanks to my agent, Marc Gerald, for doing what you said you could do . . . help me realize my dream. Special thanks to my editor, Janete Scobie. Thanks for showing me the ropes and patiently leading the way through this strange new world. Much thanks to my publicist, Mardessa Smith, for being in my corner from the very beginning.

To anyone I may have missed or left out unintentionally, thank you, thank you, thank you. Be blessed!

Much love,
Electa

When people show you who they are, believe them.

—Maya Angelou

Prologue

What's love got to do with it? What's love but a secondhand emotion? Tina Turner hit it right on the money with that song. I can picture her now sashaying across the stage with those long legs and that wild, sexy hair flying all over the place as she bellows out those lyrics straight from the heart. Lord knows, she could be the spokeswoman for that song because being married to Ike was no walk through the daisies.

It's amazing how when we are young and haven't experienced life yet, songs are listened to for the beat and the rhythm. It's only later, when we are older and wiser, that we listen to and relate to the lyrics behind the songs. We can relate because we have been there and done that.

Reflecting back on the last few turbulent months of my life, I realize I have changed. Really, I had no choice but to change from a naive young woman who thought she knew it all into a mature, wiser woman. You see, I have learned that life has a way of teaching us hard lessons about love. And believe me, there are many lessons to be taught, lessons learned only by living them. You have to go through them and survive to truly understand.

Sometimes, the only way is to live life, learn from our mistakes and move on. Unfortunately, when it comes to love, for a lot of us, it takes a while longer to get to that moving on stage. A lot of us have to be taught the lesson over and over again before we finally get it. Women, throughout history, have played the fool for love. And you know what? We probably always will. It has been drilled into us from birth that to be truly happy we need a man in our life and in our bed. I'm sure I can get some amens to that.

The lessons I have learned are quite simple. *Lesson number one: The entire concept of love is a bunch of pure, one hundred percent, unadulterated bullshit.* Love doesn't conquer all or solve all our problems; if anything, love probably complicates matters. Once love comes into the picture, it totally changes things. You definitely can't live off of it when your symbol of love is beating you down.

Lesson number two: Never, never, never, I repeat, never, let a man, no matter how much you love him or he claims to love you, control your life or become your life. Before you know it, you have lost your identity and ultimately yourself. I swear on my daddy's grave that will never, ever, happen to me—AGAIN.

If I ever have children, especially a daughter, I'm going to teach her that fairy tales are just that—fairy tales. There isn't a black knight in shining armor who's going to ride into your life and love you, protect you and cherish you forever. That shit only happens in the movies. In real life, love usually comes with a price.

1   Christian

They say there comes a time in every man's life when he has to stand up and be a man. He has to make a decision that is going to affect the rest of his life. Yet there is no turning back. Well, that time has come for me. My life is now divided into "before the incident" and "after the incident."

Love can make us do some crazy shit. That little four-letter word was never in my vocabulary until recently. Hell, I am, or should I say was, one of the biggest players out there. Don't take that the wrong way. I am honest about who and what I am . . . no games, just straight-up, up-front honesty. That's what the women of the nineties want . . . right?

Don't get me wrong. I'm just not about to settle down and do the "family thing"; that is all so boring and predictable. I honestly believe that I wasn't born to be monogamous; it's not in my genes. Therefore, I'm not going to live my life based on a lie.

Like I said before, I'm straight up. I'm not about playing these bullshit games. I'm too old for that shit. I let them know right up front . . . I am *not* about commitment, falling in love, marriage, children, or the white picket fence. I'm enjoying my life to the fullest and their company at that particular moment in time. If they have any other ideas then they had better step.

But when love calls your name, you can't run away no matter how hard you try or how bad you want to. I should know because I know I tried. In fact, I thought I was running a marathon. But I fell in love with a lady who has the face of an angel and a heart of gold. Mia . . . that's her name. Mia. I think I loved her the first time

I laid eyes on her. She literally touched my heart, and I have never been the same since. No one else could ever make me feel this way.

I was in denial for a long time, trying to run from the truth, but the truth has a funny way of finding your ass. Mia is damn near perfect and I would willingly give up my life for her. That's some heavy shit coming from me, but I would with no hesitation. There is one small problem. Actually, it is quite a major problem. Mia doesn't love me. She has eyes only for my best friend, Brice—her husband.

Yeah, there comes a time when you have to do the right thing. Sometimes the right thing involves hurting people you don't want to hurt. But, hey, life is full of disappointment, betrayal and pain. I should know.

rs. Brice Matthew. Mrs. Mia Matthew. Mia Matthew. Life is good. I still can't believe I actually met, fell in love with and married my black knight in shining armor. Fairy tales do come true; I'm witness to that. Mama and Uncle Larry are always saying that I am a hopeless romantic. Yes, I cry watching sappy love stories, and yes, I want that kind of love. A love where when I see *him,* my legs tremble, my heart rate speeds up, and when I look into his eyes, I know my meaning for living. Now, that's love. I truly believe, though, that there is one special person out there for each and every one of us: a soul mate. Once you meet that person, your life is complete.

Brice . . . I love that man so much. I love everything about him, from his sexy, penetrating brown eyes, his sensuous lips that kiss my neck, my breasts and every place imaginable, to his strong hands with his long, trim fingers that know just where to stroke. . . . The list goes on and on.

Brice is everything I have ever wanted in a man and more. I have to pinch myself every night before I go to sleep and every morning when I wake up to make sure I'm not dreaming. I know, I know, he has me whipped. And you'd best believe I love every minute of it and every inch of him.

Don't get me wrong, now. Brice is not perfect. Oh, man, Brice is by no means perfect. He has a fiery temper that he can't control, he has a possessive nature, and he loves me too much. Yeah, too much. Sometimes it's suffocating. I'll get into that later. For now, I am going to continue lying here basking in the afterglow of good—no great—lovemaking while I watch my husband sleep like a newborn baby.

Mia is the love of my life. I have always dreamed of marrying a woman like her. She is beautiful, intelligent, sexy and everything a man could want in a woman. I wanted to have the type of marriage that my parents had when I was growing up. After thirty-plus years of marriage, they are still kicking it and still very much in love.

Mia is younger than me, eight years to be exact. She's only twenty-two years old. That concerned me in the beginning because I felt that she needed to do some more growing up, which she does, but then I realized that she was still at an age where she could be molded. I know that sounds old-fashioned and makes me sound like a male chauvinist or something, but I am none of the above. Mia has her own mind and can do whatever she wants to do—to an "extent." She is still learning what that "extent" is. My daddy didn't take any mess from his wife, my moms, and I don't intend to either. Mia thinks I am too possessive of her. I tell her that I am just being a man, and I intend to wear the pants in my family. She can learn that the easy way or the hard way.

Before I met Mia, my boy Christian and me were out there. And I do mean out there. We were never at a loss for women and pussy. There is something about a man in uniform that turns a lot of women on. Women love Marines. And I love women. If Mia ever knew some of the shit that we did, she probably would never have married me. I can't even believe some of the things that we did to get some. But those days are gone for me. I am totally committed to Mia.

When I want some, all I have to do is roll over and spread her legs wide and she is always willing and ready. All my years of experience have paid off, because I can do some shit to Mia that drives her out of her mind. She'll be screaming, arching that tiny back with her perky breasts begging to be stroked, calling out my name and coming in her panties before I can even get it in good. Then she'll have those long, slim legs wrapped around my waist so that she can take all of me inside of her. Yeah, Mia is definitely dick whipped; she totally gives her body to me with no inhibitions.

4 Christian

The day and circumstances under which I met Mia are permanently etched in my mind. It was a day that would change everything that I believed in, and for that matter, everything I didn't believe in. I received a phone call from my boy Brice, who had recently returned from a thirty-day leave, and he asked me to come over for one of his infamous cookouts. Brice is my best friend; we have been best friends since we were around six or seven years old.

Actually, he is more like a brother than a friend. I have his back and he always has mine. We have been through a lot of heavy shit together, but through thick and thin he has been there for me. In high school, we were dubbed the "Two Musketeers"; when you saw me you saw him. We rarely let anyone into our little circle. When my mother died in a car accident during my sophomore year of high school, it was Brice who asked his parents to take me in.

My father, well, I have never known my father. I think during my entire lifetime I have seen him three, maybe four times. I could walk down the street and look him straight in the face and not even know that I was looking at my dad. That's really sad because, personally, I think that if you can pull out your dick and fuck, then you should be man enough to take care of any babies you make. A boy needs his father to show him how to be a man. But since my dad wasn't much of a man, I guess I didn't miss anything. Anyway, that's water under the bridge. I'm thirty years old.

On the other hand, my mother, Emily, was everything to me. Even though we didn't have much, we had each other. My older brother, Randy, had been killed by a stray bullet years earlier. My moms worked hard, and I didn't have the newest or most fashion-able clothes, but I always had a hot meal on the table and clean clothes on my back. Moms refused to let me quit school and find a job to help out around the house. House, well, we didn't have a house, but it was a home. You see, I am a product of the projects, and everything you have heard and seen is true. In reality, it is probably worse. Living there makes you grow up fast and without any disil-lusions about life. Moms made a home for me out of that four-room apartment, though.

I sometimes wonder how Brice and I even became friends. Brice was the total opposite of me. He grew up with both parents. His mother, Vivica, is a retired schoolteacher, and his father, Richard, is a retired carpenter. I loved to visit him and spend the night at his house even though it showed me just how little Moms and I actu-ally had. Brice was and is all the things that I wanted to be. He was popular, athletic, handsome and charming. The women loved, and still do love, Brice. Of course, me being his best friend made me popular also.

After Moms passed, I thought I was going to lose my fucking mind. How could this happen to me? First Randy, then Moms, and my father might as well have been dead. My grades started to drop, I lost weight and didn't care about myself or anyone else for that matter. I think that was when I decided to never love anyone again, because love can vanish so quickly and the hurt and pain lasts for-ever. I shielded myself to never feel that way again. Today, if a woman gets too close . . . I'm history. I'm gone!

Brice helped me out of my depression as only Brice could. When I moved in with him and his family, we ended up sharing his room. It was a bedroom that could have been considered large for one person, but with my arrival and clutter it seemed like there was never enough room. Yet Brice never complained even once to me.

I was lying on my back staring into space with the lights off, which is something I was doing quite often, when Brice entered our room.

"Man, get off your lazy ass and stop feeling sorry for yourself."

I continued to lie there as if I hadn't heard him. That was easy for him to say, he still had his mother and father.

He said disgustedly, "Christian, just look at yourself! Would your Moms want you to exist like this? No, I don't think so."

Brice noticed that he had gotten my attention with the mention of my moms. So he continued. "Man, your Moms is gone physically, but you still have her here in your heart and in your memories. You will never lose that. No one can ever take that away from you."

I was still lying there like a zombie, but I was seeing a new side to my friend. This was a man who could get a freshman girl at school who was half out of her mind over him to give him a blow job in the bathroom at a Friday-night party and act like he had never seen her before on Monday morning at school. This was the same man who would bet me twenty dollars that he would fuck this girl or that girl at the basketball game in the backseat of his car and then tell me all the intimate details of how tight she was, how she was moaning and begging for more or how he made her suck him off.

"Life is for the living, and you have plenty of people who love, support and care about you. Christian, get over it! Emily would want you to have a life. Make her proud."

I still didn't react or move or even indicate that I had heard anything that he had said to me. As he exited the room, I heard him say, "Christian, I'm not going to give up on you."

I lay there and closed my eyes as silent, hot tears slowly slid down my cheeks. That was the beginning of a new life and the ending to an old one.

Okay, it has almost been a year. God, time flies by so quickly. Has it really almost been a year that I have been Mrs. Brice Matthew? Brice promised my mother, Uncle Larry and me that he would help me enroll in college after our first year together. I have only a few more credits to go before I can receive my bachelor's degree. Hopefully, one day soon, I'll be somebody's elementary-school teacher.

When I married Brice, I had to drop out of college in order to move to North Carolina, where he is stationed. The sacrifices love will make us take. Mama and Uncle Larry made him promise them that he would encourage me to finish school, though. With or without Brice's encouragement, I know that I will receive that piece of paper. Having a college degree and teaching has always been a dream that I intend to make reality.

Brice didn't want me to work or go to school or do anything our first year together except be his wife and lover. That was cool because it was a huge adjustment for me to make. I came straight from my mama's house and college into this new role. It's like I went from being a little girl to an adult by just crossing state lines. Sometimes I feel like I'm playing house with a grown man. Not only did I get a husband, but also I had to relocate to a new state, and to a military community at that. A military community is so close-knit, it's like a town within a town.

I left behind all my family and friends to start a new life. I had to get used to Brice's likes and dislikes, and there are many. To say the very least, it hasn't been smooth sailing from day one, but I love my man so much.

Sometimes, hell, a lot of times, Brice treats me like a child and I have to remind him that I'm not one. Take last night for example. He was actually home for a change, which is rare. I am alone a lot because Brice travels for the military as a recruiter, and I haven't made any friends yet. Sometimes Christian will come over and keep me company.

Anyway, we were sitting on this tacky green sofa that Brice owned before we got married—I couldn't convince him to get rid of it—watching some show on TV.

As I snuggled closer under him and his warm embrace, he caressed my breasts and I asked, "Brice, when are you going to get the paperwork so that I can register for fall classes at State?"

"Mia, I wish you would quit bugging me about those damn papers. I'm going to get them for you. Okay?"

"Baby, you have been saying that for the last week. I need to look at the catalogue and decide what I need to take."

"Why do you have to rush back to school, anyway? We barely spend anytime together as it is. Staying out another quarter isn't going to kill you."

By now I have broken away from his embrace, and I'm staring at him. "I knew that you would try this shit, Brice! I'm ready to go back. You promised my mama, Uncle Larry and me. It's not my fault that you are away all the time." I pouted. "I promise that my studying won't interfere with us."

"It had better not," he said as he pulled me back into his strong arms and continued to stroke my nipples and breasts as he unbuttoned my shirt.

I pulled away from him abruptly, which startled him. I was determined to get a definite answer before things went any farther.

"Oh, come on, baby," he said in a husky, sexy voice. "You can't stop now. I want you."

I asked, "When are you bringing me the papers?" as I started to button up my open shirt.

"Oh, it's like that? You won't give me any until I promise to bring you the info?"

Before I could even open my mouth to respond, Brice was all over me. He grabbed me by the arm and pushed me down on the sofa and managed to get my shirt and bra off in record time. He had his full weight on me and was looking down at me with lust-filled eyes.

"Mia, I've told you that I am the man in this house and I don't play these little games that you like to play so much. Do you hear me?"

By now I was screaming for him to get off of me. I weigh roughly 120 and Brice is a solid 230. He's a big man.

"Do you hear me? Answer me, Mia."

I nodded my head, and Brice released some of his weight. He glanced at me for a few moments and then started caressing my cheek with his right hand while his left hand touched me between the thighs and gently rubbed.

"Did I hurt you?"

I shook my head without looking at him. He rose on one elbow and told me, "Get up and pull off your panties and jeans, baby."

"Brice, I don't want to. Leave me alone."

"Mia, don't let me tell you again to pull them off and get over here."

I did, he proceeded to screw me, and the next day he handed over the paperwork.

6   Brice

What was up with that shit from last night? Mia is always causing more drama than is necessary. I was going to get the damn info she needed to register for her classes. I thought that she would love to have another quarter off; hell, I know I would love to lay around the house all day, go shopping almost every day with someone else's money and just take it easy. But I don't have that luxury; someone has to be the breadwinner in this household.

Mia can be so stubborn at times. I know that I scared her slightly last night, but she has to learn that she can't play her games with me. Sometimes she acts just like a child, and children have to be disciplined once in a while. I wear the pants in my household, and what I say goes. My daddy once told me that the secret to his and Moms's long-lasting marriage is that Moms knew who was the boss.

Daddy said, "Son, from the get-go, let her know who's the man. It's good for them to be just a little afraid of you. That way you don't have to tap that ass so often to get your point across."

I looked at him standing there trying to tell me how to be a real man and boasting about the times he had slapped Moms around. Well, he didn't exactly tell me that part, but I still remembered those incidents from when I was younger. Once I got older, once they got older, it didn't happen as much. But I still remember those heated arguments over money, the house, whatever. They never fought in front of me. It was always upstairs in their bedroom, behind closed doors.

Daddy would start screaming at Moms about something, and then Moms, with her meek and mild-mannered ways, would start crying. Daddy couldn't stand that. He couldn't stand to see her cry. I would hear his muffled, deep voice asking her how she could be so stupid. Then there would be more crying and loud slaps; the sound of a hand making contact with flesh. Moms would be pleading with him to stop hitting her and promising him that it, whatever it was, wouldn't happen again.

Later that night I would hear sounds of ecstasy, moaning and screeching bedsprings going to town late into the night. I don't know if Moms had sex with him willingly, but daddy got his. My daddy is a big man. He stands over six-four, and Moms is five-one— a petite, classy lady. The next morning Moms would serve breakfast with long sleeves on or make up some excuse about her swollen face as if nothing had happened. Daddy would sip his coffee and read the morning paper.

Now, don't get me wrong. I would never hit or physically hurt Mia. I love her too much to harm her. Even last night, yeah, I was pissed, and I wanted her to quit riding me about school, but I didn't hit her. Anyway, what I laid on her had her thinking of nothing else. By the time we were finished making love, Mia was moaning, crooning and begging me to stick her some more.

Let me tell you how I met Mia and made her my wife. Like I said earlier, my wife is a beautiful lady. She's petite, kind of like my Moms. She's not skinny; I mean she has a shape, an ass and breasts. She's about five-six to my six-three. I got my daddy's height. Mia has pretty almond-shaped brown eyes and shoulder-length hair, which she wears pulled back in a ponytail the majority of the time. When she walks into a room you can't help but notice her. Mia projects confidence, warmth and beauty. She has a kind word and a smile for everyone.

I was on a thirty-day military leave. I hadn't had any time off in quite a while. I decided to go home and visit the folks for a month and just chill. My first week back in Georgia I met Mia at a cookout that one of my cousins threw at his house. My cousin Reggie and his wife, Gloria, threw down. They had the chicken, ribs and steaks slamming. And Gloria outdid herself with the potato salad, beans, desserts . . . You get the picture.

I had already made my first round with the food and was working on my second or third beer. Meanwhile, the fellows and me joked around and played some serious cards out back. When I glanced up, I saw Gloria walking our way with this beautiful woman who was dressed casually in denim shorts that showed off her sexy brown legs and a red halter top that exposed her flat, silky stomach. Through the flimsy material of her halter I got the distinct outline of her perfect, ample round breasts. She had on brown sandals, and her toenails were painted bright red. When she threw back her head to laugh at something Gloria said, that smile was dazzling. She had her hair pulled back in a ponytail; this helped to highlight her beautiful, high cheekbones and her eyes. Mia was simply breathtaking, and I couldn't take my eyes off her. I didn't even realize that I was holding my breath in awe until they arrived at our table.

Gloria stared in my direction with a slight smile of amusement on her face and said, "Brice, I wanted to introduce you to our neighbor Mia. She's home on summer break from college."

"Mia, this is Brice, who is also home on leave from the military."

We both smiled and said our hellos. Mia held out her hand, and when our hands touched . . . I swear I felt a volt of electricity surge through me.

Mia smiled her electrifying smile and asked, "Brice, what have you been up to?"

"Not too much. Mostly chillin' and doing some painting around my parents' house."

"You mean there isn't a girlfriend somewhere that you came back to visit?" she asked, boldly flirting.

"Noooo. What about you? You didn't bring your little boyfriend with you today?"

"No, I'm currently available, and I'm not a little girl, by the way."

"No, how old are you?"

By now everyone at the table was looking and grinning at this encounter taking place.

"How old are *you*?" Mia asked.

"I'm old enough to show you some things."

"I bet you are," she stated as she and Gloria walked off.

I saw her glance back my way a couple of times as they talked to another group of people. As for me, I was hooked. I couldn't even finish the card game. I had to find out more about Mia with her sexy self.

My cousin Reggie filled me in on all the details. He said that Mia was their next-door neighbor. She was about twenty-two years old and was a good girl, from what he had seen. You know, she didn't mess around with a lot of men. She kept pretty much to herself when she was home. Her mother was a recovering alcoholic, and he didn't know where the father was. Mia was going to school to be a teacher and was outgoing, outspoken and caring.

His last comment to me was, "Man, don't dog that girl."

"What are you talking about?" I asked.

"Brice, you haven't changed, man. You know what I mean. Regardless of that flirting, Mia is really sweet. She's a good girl. Don't charm her to get some ass and end up hurting her. You can get free pussy anywhere."

"You have my intentions all wrong, my man. She seems like a nice girl. I just want to get to know her. I'm cool."

"Okay, man, if you say so."

I glanced around to see where Mia had disappeared to. I saw her over by the swing set playing with the children. I decided to get another beer, and join her. As I made my way over, I found myself getting nervous. This was new for me. I was usually confident around women. I knew then that Mia was different. I finally made my way across the lawn. I could see Mia was watching me approach out of the corner of her eye.

I had brought over two beers. "Hey, pretty lady," I said in my best Jamaican accent, "would you like a cold beer or aren't you old enough to drink?"

Mia smiled and said, "I'm old enough, but I don't drink. Sorry."

"Don't be sorry. It's rare to see that in this day and age."

We stood there for a few seconds.

"You know, you look like one of those little kids yourself," I joked as I looked into her pretty brown eyes.

"But I'm not, am I? Look, I'm twenty-two years old. Okay? Why are you so hung up on my age? How old are you?"

"Wait a minute, this conversation is not going the way I planned it. I am thirty years old and I don't have a problem with your age. I simply came over to ask a beautiful lady out. Do you have plans for later this evening?"

She hesitated. "I don't know. What do you have in mind?"

"Well, Grant Park is having a jazz concert later this evening. Would you like to go?"

Mia got right up in my face, stared up at me for a few seconds. She was so close that I could feel her breath on my face and see clearly her long black eyelashes. She said, "I have to think about it. I'll let you know." And then . . . she simply walked off and left me standing there. I stood there shaking my head because no lady had ever done that to me before.

For a moment, I was going to go out with the boys without waiting for her call, but I ended up waiting around my parents' house for the rest of the evening. I knew she would get my phone number from Gloria, but I wasn't so sure at first she would call. She called, and we talked briefly and agreed to attend the concert. When I picked Mia up at her house, she met me at the door and hurried me to the car. She was stunning. Mia had changed into a multicolored short set. The kind that had baggy-fitting walking shorts with a bikini top and an unbuttoned shirt over that. She had the shirt off, so I had a full view of her ample, full chest. All I could think about was getting the opportunity to touch her breasts.

We had so much fun at the concert. The bands were good, the atmosphere was festive and it even cooled down with a slight breeze. Mia had brought a beach blanket, which we spread out in a grassy area to listen to the cool jazz sounds that were mellowing everyone out. We talked some. Mia had a good head on her shoulders. She asked me a lot of questions about the military, which I answered as honestly as possible.

We flirted back and forth. I soon discovered that Mia's flirting was innocent. At one point, she was laying her head in my lap as if we had known each other forever. I looked at her talking on and on, and I leaned down to give her a kiss. She quickly jumped up before it could happen and continued talking about school and North Carolina. By now I wanted her like I had never wanted anyone before. I was literally about to explode.

After we had gathered up the beach towel and our soda cans, we decided to walk around for a while before leaving for home. After putting everything into my car, we walked hand in hand, just talking about everything and nothing. We talked and laughed as if we had known each other all our lives. Everyone was right; Mia was really sweet.

The moment of truth finally arrived. I dropped her off at her tiny brick home. I had already decided against trying anything with her, but I did want at least a kiss from those luscious lips. As we were walking to her door, she was telling me how much she enjoyed the evening. Mia got to the last step and was unlocking her door as I was turning to leave when she said . . .

"Brice, wait." She walked the short distance to me, looked intensely at me and leaned up and kissed me. For a moment I was caught off guard, but I soon recovered. It was a sweet kiss that made me want more. I could feel her petite body pressed up against mine with her nipples, which were now erect, rubbing up against my chest. We broke away from the kiss and looked into each other's eyes. I could tell that Mia wanted more. Hell, I wanted more. She was kinda moving her groin up against mine. There was plenty of electricity and heavy breathing going on.

"Good night," Mia said as she turned and walked into her house and closed the door behind her. I slowly drove home and took a long, cold shower. I climbed into my old bed, the one I slept in as a child, and thought confused, frustrated, but happy thoughts of Mia.

The following morning, I woke up bright and early with Mia on my mind. On impulse, I decided to give her a wake-up call and wish her a good morning. I was quite disappointed, to my surprise, when a sleepy voice stated that she had already left for work at the day care center. For the rest of the morning and afternoon I worked around the house doing much-needed fix-it work and minor repairs. Daddy wasn't in good health and couldn't do some of the things he used to do. Things around the house had fallen into a state of disarray.

By the time five o'clock rolled around, I had showered and put on some clean clothes and decided to give Mia another call. She was there this time and seemed surprised to hear from me. I couldn't figure this one out.

"Hey, baby girl, what's up?"

"I told you, don't—"

"I know, don't call you baby girl."

"That's right. I'm all woman, or can't you tell?" she asked jokingly.

I responded with a laugh. "You haven't given me anything to prove that you are all woman yet."

"What do I need to give you?"

"If I have to tell you that, then you must be a little girl."

"Anyway, who said I was giving you some? Seriously, Brice, I'm tired. Tired of running after screaming children all day."

"Why don't you let me take you out for a quiet dinner and stimulating conversation?" I asked.

Mia agreed, and I told her good-bye until later that evening. As soon as I drove up, Mia came out of the house and jumped in the car. This time she had on a bright red sundress, no bra, with slingback red shoes and bright red fingernail and toenail polish. She was looking sexy as usual. I was kidding her about her mother. "Do you have a mother or are you holding her tied and bound inside the house?" Mia sorta laughed and changed the subject, and so I dropped it as well.

Dinner was at the Cheesecake Factory. The food was good, but Mia ate like a bird. That was all right, though, because I got the chance to see her lovely face again. Mia was like a ray of sunshine. After dinner, she wasn't ready to go home yet, and neither was I, so she suggested that we go to the local park and talk.

Once at the park, I drove into a somewhat secluded area and turned off the ignition. Mia didn't want to walk; she just wanted to talk. She told me all about her mother and how hard it was for her to deal with her as a recovering alcoholic. There were good and bad days for both of them. She said that her mother had never gotten over the death of her husband, Mia's father. She almost drank herself into an early grave. Roles were reversed, and Mia was more like a mother to her mother for most of her teenage years. She said if it hadn't been for her uncle Larry, her father's brother, she didn't know how she would have made it. I could tell that this subject was causing her great pain.

I didn't know what to say, so I took her in my arms and held her and said, "It'll be okay. It'll be okay. You are safe with me now."

It seems like we sat like that for the longest time, with me holding her and rubbing her back. No words were spoken. None were necessary. It was a comfortable silence. I wanted to shield her from the world.

When Mia had composed herself somewhat, she sat back up and looked at me. She was making me uncomfortable with her stare.

I said, "What?"

"Nothing. You just surprised me. I didn't know that you could be so caring. Thank you."

That comment caught me off guard. I responded, "What do you mean by that?"

"Oh, I have done my homework. I've heard some pretty wild stories about you and somebody named Christian. And you didn't come across as the caring, gentle type."

"Is that a fact? Now, who told you all that?"

"It doesn't matter. I just know."

"Then why do you want to be with me if I'm all that?"

Mia shrugged, deep in thought. "I don't know. Maybe I like excitement and danger," she said laughingly.

"May I kiss you?" Hell, where did that come from? I had never asked a lady for a kiss. I took what I wanted.

She nodded. I gently touched her chin and pulled Mia into an embrace. Mia tilted her head. Next thing I knew, it was like fireworks on the Fourth of July. Seriously, her kiss, her touch, sent chills up and down my spine. I could tell Mia felt it too, because the kiss became more passionate. I had slid over to her side of the seat, and she climbed into my lap, straddling me with her legs. I started squeezing her breasts through her sundress, and Mia was moaning and moving up and down on me. I managed to get her dress unbuttoned, and I pulled the top portion down to release her breasts. They were not too large or too small. Her nipples were erect, and she was still doing that moving up and down motion.

I cupped her breasts with both hands and started rubbing them, and finally I put a nipple in my mouth and started sucking. This was driving her crazy. The more I sucked, the harder I sucked, the louder she moaned. My fingers had managed to pull up her dress and they were moving in and out between her silky thighs. She was so wet, moist and hot. I continued to move one, then two and three fingers inside of her. She opened her trembling legs even wider to receive me. I was coming in my pants. Mia had me so hot.

"Wait, Brice. Wait . . . I'm sorry, I can't," she said as she pushed me away, got up and pulled down and buttoned up her sundress.

"What the hell do you mean, you can't? You can if you want to. Baby, I'm a grown man, and I have needs. I can't deal with this little schoolgirl shit. I need a woman."

"I'm sorry," she said as she looked at me with sad, disappointed eyes. "I'm just not ready to give myself to you like that."

I was back on the driver's side, looking out the window, trying to calm down.

"Look, just take me home, Brice."

"Mia, I'm sorry. If you aren't ready, then you just aren't ready. I'll be more patient. Okay?"

She smiled a sweet smile. I held her some more and took her home about an hour later.

This girl had my nose wide open! I had never been there before. This was definitely a first. Christian wasn't going to believe this. This knowledge still didn't help the hard-on that I had. I had had one for two days now. I had to get some relief. I drove over to an old flame's house after I dropped off Mia. I know, call me a dog. Janice was just what I needed to give me some release. She was willing and ready, even though she had heard that I was "messing with" that girl over on Fifth Street. She didn't care. She just wanted some.

I fucked Janice like I had never fucked before. I was pounding out all my pent-up frustrations into that pussy. She didn't know what hit her. I could have broken my dick off in her. With women like her, I don't make love. I fuck. You lay down like a whore, I treat you like the whore you are. With Janice, I didn't have to step to her with flowers or wining and dining; just with what was between my legs.

I thrusted and sucked and stroked like there was no tomorrow. I was trying to satisfy an animal need. I may have been a little too rough with Janice, because she tried to pull away a couple of times, but I pushed her back down and pulled her fat ass back up to greet and receive my throbbing rod. I was sucking those breasts and pinching those huge nipples like I had two large melons to devour.

Later, I had her on her hands and knees with that big ass stuck up in the air as I laid it on her. Her pussy started making that sucking sound, she started screaming like a banshee and it was all over. Much later, I woke up wanting more. I pushed her head down to my already-erect penis. She was shaking her head. "Brice, I don't suck dick." I told her that after all she had done tonight and all I had done to her, what difference did that make.

Janice continued to protest, but I didn't relent. She looked at me for just a second, long enough to realize I was serious, and I looked at her with . . . you had better get your ass down there and go to work before I tap that ass. I opened my legs so that she wouldn't have any problem taking it *all* in. Soon I had her bobbing her head up and down as she worked my jimmy to yet another release. At that point, I let go of her hair and stopped rubbing her breasts and laid back down into another exhausted sleep. Early the next morning, I removed myself from her embrace, quietly walked out of her apartment and headed home.

For my remaining days at home, Mia and I were inseparable when she wasn't working at the day care center. She even called in sick a few times when I begged her to spend the entire day with me. Yeah, Mia was constantly on my arm. We did everything together.

All this time, Mia still hadn't given herself to me. She would only let me kiss her; she said anything else gave me the wrong idea. I finally "got the draws" as they say, close to my final week in Georgia. I had the most explosive orgasm that I have ever had in my entire life.

Mia, myself, Moms and Daddy were all sitting around my parents' mahogany dining room table ready to throw down on some serious soul food. Moms still loved to cook these huge Sunday dinners that we always sat down to directly after returning from morning service at our church. Today, Moms had really gone out of her way and thrown down. We feasted on collard greens and ham hocks, green beans, chicken, baked ham, fried corn, corn on the cob, corn bread, fried okra, potato salad and fresh, homemade potato pie.

Moms had been begging and begging to meet the young lady who was taking up so much of my time. When I told her Mia was going to church with us and could come to dinner afterwards, Moms stayed up late Saturday night preparing dishes and making sure everything was perfect. You see, even though I am thirty years old, I had never, ever, brought a woman home to meet my parents.

Moms always said she "wanted grandchildren before she was too old to enjoy and spoil them."

I must admit that I actually enjoyed the church service. The pastor, Reverend Penn, preached an uplifting sermon about the institution of marriage and the family structure, and the choir was off the hook. They even had me standing up and clapping. I also had the opportunity to see a lot of people whom I hadn't seen in years. Mia was as beautiful as ever, sitting by my side. She was conservatively dressed today in a navy and white suit with matching earrings and pearls. She wore her shoulder-length hair down in cascading curls that framed her face. She had on just a hint of makeup and was dazzling. Mia held my hand during most of the service, and I felt her glancing at me a few times with a smile on her lovely face.

After the church service was over, we headed back home. I could tell that Mia was nervous about meeting my parents at first. She was not her usual talkative self on the drive home. Church had been somewhat of a diversion because all she had to do was sit and give her full attention to the preacher, but after arriving at my house, she changed into her usual attire of shorts, T-shirt and sandals and was holding her own. She even helped Moms heat up the food. I also noticed Daddy checking her out a couple of times.

"So, Mia, why did you decide to major in education?" Moms inquired.

"I have always loved children and seeing the wonder light up in their eyes when they learn something new. I know that it doesn't pay a lot, but I feel that this is my way to give back to the community."

Moms stated, "It's really a different system out there now, with a new breed of children from when I first started out. These kids don't respect you like they used to. They will curse you out and run over you if you let them. But there are the special few who want to learn. I was there for them."

It was amazing to see the two women that I loved most interact. Yeah, I said it. I loved Mia. I had realized that a few days earlier. I loved her . . . I had never felt this way about a woman, ever.

When dinner was over and everybody was stuffed after having seconds at Moms's insistence, Moms and Mia washed the dishes together. I could hear them in the kitchen laughing and giggling like two schoolgirls. This made me feel happy for some reason. Meanwhile, Daddy and I were in the den watching the baseball game. Well, actually I was watching as Daddy dozed on and off. Finally, Mia and Moms came back into the den to join us. Mia was rubbing her eye saying that something, some lint or speck of dirt, was in her eye, irritating it. She excused herself to the bathroom.

When she hadn't returned a few minutes later, I went to check on her. She was in the upstairs bathroom, the one at the end of the hallway, leaning over the sink, pulling her eyelid down when I found her.

"Hey, did you get it?" I asked.

"No, I don't see anything." She pouted.

"Here, get up on the counter and let me have a look," I said as I lifted her up easily and looked into her eye to remove a small speck of dirt.

I showed it to her and asked, "What would you do without me?"

After I had gotten it out, we kinda stood there smiling at each other because we were not ready to give up that small closeness. We hadn't been alone together all day. She was sitting on the counter and I was standing between her legs.

"You really impressed my folks today. I can tell that they like you." Mia smiled because that pleased her.

I bent down to give her a kiss, and she pulled me into her with her ankles and gave me this deep, passionate kiss.

I pulled away and said, "Don't start something that you can't finish, little girl."

She smiled and said, "Who said I was going to stop?"

We started kissing again, and I started rubbing her breasts through her T-shirt. I could tell that this was turning her on and getting her hot.

"I want to feel your hands on my skin, baby," she said as she pulled up her shirt to expose her breasts.

I proceeded to take off her shirt and bra and started sucking her nipples until they were sticking out like two blackberries ready to be plucked, and she was moaning and moving around on the counter with a look of pure ecstasy on her face. Mia started unzipping my shorts and pulling them down around my ankles with great urgency. It didn't matter that my parents were waiting for us downstairs. That only added to the thrill and excitement of the moment.

"I'm ready, Brice. I want to feel you inside of me, baby. Give me some now." She said this as she looked at my penis in awe and started stroking it up and down. By now, I was trying to get her shorts and panties off, but I wasn't going to put it in yet. I was going to make her wait like she had made me wait.

When her clothes were off and on the floor, I stuck my finger in, and she was so wet and hot. She let out this loud moan, and when I inserted a second and third finger, I thought she would go out of her mind. This entire time I was still sucking and kissing her neck and breasts. I was enjoying this because she wanted it so bad. By the time I entered her, she was soaking wet. I stuck it in with one quick dip. She sucked in her breath and took it all and started meeting my thrusts with the grinding of her hips. Slow, then fast. Up and down. Around and around.

Most women are a little afraid of my dick. Don't laugh. I am dead serious. To put it mildly, I am well endowed; above average, so to speak. They freak out when they first see it and think that I am going to rip them apart or something. So I was being especially gentle with Mia; I didn't want to hurt or frighten her.

"Baby, I don't break. I'm not that fragile. Give it to me. I want to feel *all* of you."

"Are you sure?"

She nodded. I gave her what she wanted; Mia took all of me over and over. She was moaning and grunting so loudly that I had to put my hand over her mouth so that my parents wouldn't hear all the noise she was making. Mia was so wet that my dick kept slipping out. Finally I turned her around so that I could enter her from behind and fondle her breasts at the same time. It was erotic watching ourselves in the bathroom mirror as we made love. I could see every facial expression and movement that Mia made. I was laying it on her. . . . We both came at the same time. It was . . . it was . . . I can't even describe it. I had never had an orgasm like that before. We looked at each other with these goofy grins, quietly redressed and went back into the den and rejoined my folks, who were both quietly snoring in their separate recliners.

After everything I had seen for myself and heard about Mia, I knew that I had to have her, and I didn't mean as a girlfriend, either. I couldn't live without her now, and I didn't see myself in a long-distance relationship with her. I wanted her in my bed, in my arms when I closed my eyes at night. I only had one week left before I was scheduled to return to North Carolina and my military duties, which required a lot of travel on my part. I didn't know what I was going to do. . . .

For the first time in my life, I followed my heart. I had gotten over the age difference between us. Mia was intelligent and grown up most of the time. She acted silly and childish only occasionally, and then I would have to remind myself that she was still pretty much a child. She was fiery and independent; that was fine as long as she knew I was the man. That she would learn. She hadn't been out there too much sexually. She told me that she had only slept with three other guys. That pleased me, because she was still kinda pure, and I definitely knew what she liked and how to please her. I had slept with her two other times since that Sunday, and each time she was begging me for more. She couldn't get enough.

Everyone was telling me not to hurt Mia. She was so sweet. Hell, who did they think I was? Yeah, I had been out there for a while. Hey, I was single, and pussy is pussy, but now I was ready to settle down and do the right thing with a lady I loved. My "dog days" were over.

So, to make a long story short, I proposed to Mia at the spur of the moment. I didn't even have a ring yet. Later, I gave her my grandmother's engagement ring. I just spoke from the heart, and she hesitated only a second before throwing her arms around me screaming yes, yes, yes. After that, everything went by in a haze. My parents took over from there, and arrangements were made. We had a small, simple ceremony with only our immediate families in attendance. Mia was beautiful. We married on a Saturday and were back in North Carolina on Monday morning as man and wife. I promised her a honeymoon in the late fall. I would make it up to her.

7   Christian

There is always one point in time for everyone that changes their view on life forever. We never know that it is taking place until we look back years later and say, "Yeah, that was when I started to change." For me, I changed when my mother died, when my heart froze. I know that for a fact. The second point in time, even though I didn't know it then, was when I met Mia. My heart started to defrost.

Anyway, I received a phone call from Brice inviting me over for one of his infamous cookouts. He said that he was inviting a few associates and their spouses. He wanted to catch up on what had been going on. We chatted for a while longer, and he didn't mention anything out of the ordinary that had happened on his vacation. I did notice that he seemed extremely happy, though. I showered, dressed in blue jeans and a T-shirt and headed over. We lived within two blocks of each other.

Once I got there, things were already in full swing. The mouthwatering barbecue smells met me at the door, and empty beer cans were overflowing the trash can near the patio door entrance. I said hello to a few familiar faces and made my way over to Brice, who was standing by the grill, grinning like the cat that ate the canary as he saw me approaching.

He said, "Christian, my man. What's up?" as he gave me a handshake and a brotherly hug.

"Nothing much. Have I missed out on something? Did you win the lottery and not tell me? You look good, man! Relaxed and happy."

"Christian, brace yourself; I feel like I *have* won the lottery."

"What are you talking about?" I asked. I felt like I was the only one who didn't know what was going on.

"Do you need to sit down?"

"Come on, man, what's up?"

"I want you to meet my wife," he said as he pulled a stunning young lady gently by the arm from behind the grill where she had been standing.

I stood there in utter disbelief. I'm sure my mouth must have been hanging wide open.

"Hi, Christian. It is so good to finally meet you," Mia said as she gave me a big hug and a smile.

"This is a joke, right? I know my man Brice hasn't tied the knot. Not Brice."

"Christian, believe it, man. I am a different person from the one who left thirty days ago. Mia stole my heart."

Mia said, "Christian, I hope that we will become great friends. I have heard so much about you. I know that you are like a brother to Brice." And again she gave me that dazzling smile.

Even after Brice filled me in on all the details and apologized that everything happened so quickly that I couldn't attend the ceremony, I still couldn't believe it. But then, on the other hand, I guess I could. Brice wasn't like me exactly in the relationship department. I wasn't looking for love or marriage. Brice was. He always said that once he found the right lady, a classy lady like his Moms, he would settle down. I guess up until that point he had never found the right woman, even though he had been through quite a few because he loved himself some women. A lot of local women were going to be heartbroken.

As I nursed my beer, I observed Mia and Brice. I admit, they made a stunning couple. Mia was beautiful in a sexy, innocent sort of way, if that is possible. She was petite, but still fine. Mia was probably about five-three. She had beautiful brown, smooth, flawless skin with thick, shoulder-length hair that was pulled back into a ponytail tied with a red, white and blue hair clip. And from the striped red top with no bra that she wore with denim shorts and sandals, it looked like she had a body that was going on. The more beer that was consumed the more leering eyes I noticed checking out her ample chest and long, slim legs. Brice must've noticed it too, because later on Mia came back out with a bra and Marine T-shirt on. I guess he persuaded her to change.

Brice, on the other hand, was tall, solidly built and had strong, chiseled features, a look that broke a lot of hearts. He also carried himself with an arrogance and domineering presence that intimidated a lot of people, but Mia appeared to bring out another side in him.

Later, after most of the crowd had left and Brice and I were sitting in two of his lawn chairs, finishing off another beer, he asked me what I thought of her. Mia was inside, in the kitchen, trying to clean up some of the mess.

"You are a lucky man," I stated. "Mia is beautiful and intelligent, and it is obvious that she loves you."

Mia and I had talked briefly earlier, and every other word out of her mouth was "Brice this" or "Brice that." She was head over heels in love with him. I was truly happy for my partner.

8 Mia

Today has not been a good day for me. Sure, I'm taking two courses at the university, but that still doesn't occupy my day. Most of the time I am so bored. You can only watch so much TV. Brice didn't want me to take a full schedule because he wanted me here for him, for us. I compromised because taking two courses was better than none, and I need only a few more credits to graduate. Brice wants me here for him, yet half the time he is out of town.

We have been married for a little over a year, and I still don't fit in here. I'm not military; I'm just married to a Marine. To make matters worse, I don't think Brice wants me to have any friends. He wants me all to himself. I keep trying to tell Brice that, but he won't listen to me. He can be so bullheaded at times. Going to the university is a much-needed diversion because I'm meeting people who aren't military.

Brice is trying his best to make me into this little homemaker. On the days when he is in town, he expects dinner on the table when he walks through the door. He said that that was the way his mother always did it when he was growing up. I told him that I wasn't his mother, and he just looked at me. I even have to take cooking lessons from this older lady in town, Mrs. Jackson. She is always shaking her head when we cook, like I am a lost, hopeless cause.

As I said earlier, Brice is very bullheaded, domineering and possessive . . . so a lot of times I find myself biting my tongue just to keep the peace because I love him so much. He means well and this is a learning process for both of us. God, is it a learning process! I know that he gets stressed out at work, but he doesn't have to take it out on me. He has to learn to control his temper. Just the other day, I was ready for class, about to walk out the door, when he made me go back and change my outfit. I had on a black miniskirt, black sandals and a purple midriff shirt that showed just a hint of my stomach. It was in style, everyone wore minis, everyone at State University anyway. So what was the big deal?

I had been hurriedly shoving books into my backpack when Brice approached me. "Where the hell do you think you are going dressed like that?" he asked as he roughly grabbed my arm.

"Brice, let go of me. I'm going to be late for class."

"If you don't change out of that shit, you aren't going to class."

He still hadn't released my arm and was looking at me in a mask of anger.

"What's wrong with what I have on?" I asked. I had already started wearing bras at his insistence, even though when he met me I didn't wear them.

"Mia, I don't want my wife showing off her ass to anyone but me. Now, get in there and change," he said as he pushed me towards the bedroom.

I decided I was sick of his shit and I wasn't going to move. That was a big mistake.

"Mia, get your goddamn ass into that bedroom before I rip that shit off of you myself. You are not going out of here looking like a whore." The entire time that he was saying this, he was in my face, shoving me down the hallway.

"Brice, leave me alone, dammit! You're hurting me!"

He threw me down on the bed and said, "This is your last chance, Mia. You take it off or I'll do it for you, and you don't want me to take it off."

I was lying there curled up in a ball, crying now. I slowly got up and started taking off my outfit as snot began running out my nose, and he stood, yes, stood there, watching me the entire time as I changed into jeans and a button-down shirt.

Once I was redressed he walked over to me and said, "Stop crying, Mia. You make me so angry sometimes. I don't like you showing off your stuff like that. This belongs to me." He groped and cupped my breasts through my shirt.

I pulled back and slapped his hands away.

"Oh, you know you like it, Mia," he said, laughing.

"Come here. Come here and give me some before I leave for work."

I stood there, determined to stare him down. The shit definitely wasn't funny, and I wasn't at his beck and call, ready to open wide whenever he said so.

"I said come here, Mia."

We stared each other down for a few seconds, and then I walked the short distance to him and he unbuttoned my shirt, unzipped my pants and pulled them down to my ankles. The entire time I was protesting, saying, "Brice, don't. I don't want to."

When I saw that it was useless to protest, I stood there looking at the faded green wallpaper pattern on our wall as he started vigorously sucking my breasts and inserting his fingers into me. Over and over and over. I didn't want to enjoy it or give him the satisfaction of seeing me enjoy it, but before I knew it, I was moaning and my head was thrown back in ecstasy, while he opened my legs even wider with his hands and went to work.

Brice asked, "Do you want this, baby?" in this husky, sexy voice. I shook my head no . . . noooo . . . then yes, yes, yes. "Tell me that you want it. Let me hear you say it. Tell me to fuck you. Tell me how you can't get enough of this." He placed my hand on his dick. "Oooh, baby, you feel so good . . ." I came before he even stuck it in.

Don't get me wrong, now. This was not normal behavior for Brice. Most of the time we were your average, happily married couple. When he was home, we went to the movies, shopping, to jazz clubs, you know, the usual. We spent quiet time at home wrapped in each other's arms, making love. I must admit that Brice was the best lover that I ever had. I hadn't had many, but still this man knew just what to do, how to do it and how long to do it. When I first saw his penis, I was scared out of my mind, thinking, "There is no way he can get all of that in me." But we fit perfectly, and he knows how to use it.

Brice is always teasing me, telling me I'm dick whipped. Maybe I am. I love to make love to him. He's always so gentle and sweet during those times. Well, most of the time. If he is upset with me, he'll use sex against me; either he won't give me any or he'll give me everything he has. My husband is hung, so all of that pounding and grinding can hurt, hurt bad enough to make me cry if he wants it to, and he can't stand to see me cry.

Christian has been there a lot for me when Brice isn't around. It surprises me that they are such close friends. They seem to know each other inside and out. They are devoted to each other. There is definitely a strong bond there. It still surprises me that Brice encourages Christian to spend so much time with me even though he is so jealous.

When I first met Christian at the cookout, I thought immediately that I knew why they had reputations as lady-killers. My husband is fine. He puts the capital "F" in fine, and he knows it. Christian, on the other hand, I believe, doesn't know how gorgeous he is. I may be married, but I still have eyes. Christian and Brice are about the same complexion . . . like a tanned pecan, but Christian has these sexy green eyes and a butt that says, "Touch me." He's tall, but not as tall as Brice. Christian is probably about six feet, muscular, and he has this walk that won't quit. He's also more laid-back than Brice.

I have never seen him with a girlfriend. I remember I asked Brice if Christian were gay, and he almost fell out of his chair he was laughing so hard. He said not to let Christian fool me. He said if I weren't his wife, Christian would be trying to get in my pants most definitely.

Anyhow, I don't know, when he's around me he is the perfect

gentleman. He has never said or done anything too forward. In fact, I find him to be very sincere. I find myself talking to him more and more like a girlfriend, since that is something I don't have here. And you know what, he listens. He is always telling me that I have to learn to deal with Brice's temper; he has had it for as long as he can remember. Christian said that Brice takes after his father, but he is always saying that if anyone can tame him it is me. Just give it some time.

Friday night, me and my boy Christian decided to go to this hangout in town that we used to frequent a lot. It looks like a hole in the wall from the outside, but they serve some of the best chicken wings and cold beer. It also has a mixed crowd; military hasn't taken it over yet. So there are usually quite a few nonmilitary types there. We have definitely picked up our share of booty there.

I hadn't been there since I hooked up with Mia. In fact, I hadn't been spending as much time with Christian as I used to. We had a lot of catching up to do. Mia probably saw more of him than I did. I was cool with Mia and Christian getting close. In fact, I encouraged it. I didn't want her getting too close to some of these females in town or on base for that matter. I trusted Christian and knew he wouldn't try to fuck my wife.

We had been there for about an hour just drinking and talking. It was like old times again. I even saw a few of my old "screwing partners." As soon as they saw the wedding band, they got the picture and moved on. I was proud of the fact that in the year's time I had been with Mia I hadn't had the urge or desire to cheat. I loved her too much.

I couldn't seem to get that into Brenda's head. She was this woman I used to kick it with. She had come over, interrupted our conversation and was trying to get me to go home with her.

I told her, "Baby, those days are over. I have a wife now."

"I have a husband. I don't care, Brice. You know he works the night shift. I haven't seen you in so long. And I have been asking about you, baby. I miss you."

Brenda was a little buzzed, to say the least. She sat her ass down in my lap and started to grind.

"Baby, don't you want some of this again. You know I know how you like it," she said as she grabbed my crotch.

I grabbed her by the wrist and told her if she didn't get out of my face . . . well, she had best get out of my face. She walked off, cursing.

Christian said, "Man, I told you that these women are shell-shocked over the loss of you." We both laughed at that.

"Well, you'll have to make up the difference for me."

Christian got quiet and somber for a minute. "So how is it, man? I mean, you have been balled and chained for over a year now. Do you miss the old life?"

"No."

"No, not at all?"

"Man, Mia is more than enough woman for me. Sexually, she's a little fireball."

"Don't get me wrong. I like Mia. I think she's good for you, and I definitely could get used to coming home and sleeping with that. Marriage isn't my style—but that is." I turned around in my seat to see who had caught Christian's attention as he got up and walked to the table in the corner of the bar.

I sat there and guzzled some more beer and thought about Mia. She had wanted to come with us, just to get out of the apartment, but I told her it was Men's Night Out. She pouted a little, but when I left she was watching some movie she had rented. I had to do better by her.

Meanwhile, some Prince slow jam was playing on the jukebox. Christian had gotten the lady in red to dance with him. She was wearing this hoochie outfit showing everything she had; it left nothing to the imagination. Her breasts were almost busting out, and the dress, if you wanted to call it that, barely covered her ass.

Christian glanced over at me and grinned. He liked some wild ass women. She had her arms wrapped around him like she owned the boy. When I looked up again she had her tongue stuck halfway down his throat. I swear those breasts were all up in his face like she was offering them to him on a platter, and he was palming her ass as they did their version of dirty dancing.

Christian made it back to our table, and I asked him if his "dance" was over. He smiled and said he was meeting her, Tasha, at her apartment later on. He advised me, "Man, you know I got to get some of that." I know that sounds raw, but that was how Christian and me were both kicking it over a year ago.

We talked some more, drank some more, and I was out of it when I decided that I had better go home. When I finally got the key to fit in the lock and opened the door . . . Mia was nowhere to be seen. I found a note that she left near the phone. It read: *Gone out with a girlfriend from class. Will be back soon. I love you, Mia.*

Any buzz I had immediately disappeared. I was fucking mad as hell. I was seeing red. I tore the note up into tiny shreds and sat down to wait. Yeah, I was going to wait for her ass.

Last night I was so pissed at Brice. He decided that he was going out with Christian to a so-called Men's Night Out. It was just going to be the two of them. I could have gone. But no . . . he wanted me to stay home like the good little wife that I am. I feel so old. I don't do anything anymore. I was ecstatic when Susan, a girl from class, called and invited me out with a few other people from class. We had finished finals and wanted to celebrate our few weeks of freedom. I jumped at the chance to get out. I dressed in jeans and a sweater and left a note that Brice was sure to see as soon as he walked through the door. I was going out with a girl, not a man, so everything should have been cool. Right? Wrong.

Brice hit me. He actually hit me. As soon as I walked through the door after having a great time, I spotted Brice sitting on the sofa with the TV on but the volume muted. He was staring into space, a beer in one hand and the remote in the other. It appeared that he had been sitting there for a while because he had his shirt open and the belt to his pants was unbuckled.

Right away I didn't like this. Brice had never hit me before, but in the back of my mind, I knew he was capable of it. I knew there was going to be some serious drama.

I hadn't even gotten through the door good when . . .

"Where the hell have you been?"

Brice started to stand up, and I could see that he was slightly drunk and couldn't focus clearly.

"I told you in the note that—"

"Fuck the note! Didn't I tell you to stay home?"

He slowly walked my way with his hands clenching and un-clenching into a tight fist.

"Brice, I only went out with a girlfriend from class."

"I don't give a fuck who she is. I told you to keep your ass here. See, you don't listen to me, Mia. That's your damn problem."

"Brice, please!" By now he had backed me into the front door.

Brice mocked me as he said, "Brice, please . . . Don't fucking, Brice, please, me!" Now he was in my face, screaming and looking at me with total, complete "I'm going to beat your ass" anger.

I tried to move away, but he blocked my path. There was noplace to go. I was trapped, so I started whimpering like a scared, helpless animal.

"You had better not start that crying. Do you hear me?"

I nodded my head as a ton of fresh tears streamed down my face.

"Brice, I'm sorry. If you don't want me to go out with her with-out asking, then I won't. Okay?"

I was so frightened that I would have said anything at that point.

He started pulling his belt out of his pants. "You . . . don't . . . get . . . it . . . do . . . you?" He emphasized each word by jabbing me in my ribs with his finger. "I don't want you going out with her. Pe-riod. How much plainer do I have to make it, Mia?"

"That's not fair, Brice, and you know it. I have to have a life out-side of us!" I screamed as I tried to push him out of my way.

He grabbed me and pushed me back into the door. "I'm not fin-ished talking with you. Get your ass back over here before you make me use this belt. I'll let you know when you can go."

By now I was crying out of control.

Brice grabbed my chin and forced me to look at him. "Mia, you look at me when I talk to you. Do you understand what I just told you? Look at me!" he screamed as he tightened his viselike grip on my chin.

I couldn't stand to see the man I loved treating me like this. I tried to pull away again, away from the fingers that were now pry-ing into the tender flesh on my arm.

Brice turned as if to walk away and then turned back around and slapped the shit out of me with the back of his hand. Time stood still for a moment. My eyes bucked as I fell back, hard, against the wall. I started trembling, and he stood there in amazement.

I stood up on shaky legs, bolted and ran down the hallway into our bathroom, screaming "You bastard. You bastard." I stayed in there throughout most of the night, crying. Brice had given up knocking on the door, trying to get me to come out. When it was early morning, I quietly came out when I was sure he was asleep. I got a pillow and blanket out of the hall closet and cried myself to sleep on the sofa.

Later that morning, I finally got up, bruised and aching. The apartment was dead silent and Brice was gone. When I looked in the mirror, I didn't like what I saw. My eyes were swollen from all the crying, and there was a slight bruise on my left cheek. I found a note propped up on the kitchen counter stating that Brice had left a day early to go out on recruitment. He would call me. I slowly sank down onto the cold tile floor near the refrigerator. I had never felt more alone. No apologies, no I'm sorrys. Just . . . he would call me.

I had tried calling Mia two or three times already, but no one answered. I kept getting their answering machine, and I knew she was home. Brice had called me earlier, sounding kinda strange, asking me to check on her. He said that he had called several times, but had gotten no answer. He had left several messages. That wasn't like Mia, so I got dressed and headed over.

I had knocked and knocked, called out her name and was tempted to use the spare key that I had to their apartment when the door slowly opened. Mia looked awful. Her eyes were swollen like she had been crying, and her hair was sticking up all over her head. She walked slowly and stiffly back to the sofa as she self-consciously tried to brush her hair down with her hand. Mia hadn't said anything yet. She just sat there and stared at me.

I looked back in shock. "Ahh, Mia, I was afraid something might be wrong. Brice asked me to check up on you."

"I bet he did," was all she said as she stared into space.

I was getting uncomfortable. "Look, Mia, is anything wrong? Is there anything I can do for you?"

"No thanks, Christian," she said absently. "I don't feel good. I think I'm coming down with something. I'll just go back to bed."

"Are you sure? Can I fix you something to eat or anything?"

"No, you're sweet. Thanks anyway," she said, still sitting there with no expression on her face.

"Is there anything I should tell Brice if he calls back?"

"Yeah, ask him how could he?" she said bitterly. "He'll know what I mean."

I said, "Okay. Listen, I'll check back on you later. All right?"

"Yeah, thanks, Christian."

When I quietly closed the door behind me she was still sitting in the exact same spot on the sofa, staring into space. What was that all about? That was some strange shit. As I made my way down the narrow stairs to my car, I passed one of Brice's neighbors on the stairway. He asked, "Is she all right in there?"

"Who?" I asked.

"Brice's wife. I don't know her name."

"Yeah, she's fine. I just left their apartment."

"I was wondering because last night I thought I was going to have to call the police."

"Why?" I asked, dreading the answer I knew he would give.

"Brice was beating her ass, that's why. It sounded like he was killing the poor thing. I felt sorry for her. He was screaming and cursing and she was crying. I could only imagine what he was doing to her."

He stood there looking at me as if he expected a response.

I murmured, "She's fine now."

I couldn't believe this. Brice had been fine, a little drunk maybe, but fine when I left him the night before. He was even talking about how he was going to spend more time with Mia and stop treating her like a child. I knew he wouldn't do anything to jeopardize his relationship with her. Hell yeah, he was possessive and domineering when it came to Mia, but he wouldn't hit her, would he? There had to be some sort of mistake.

Later that evening I went back over to Mia's and brought her some Chinese food for dinner. I went over uninvited because I knew if I called she either wouldn't answer the phone or would decline my offer of food. I took her some chicken chow mein with fried rice, egg-drop soup and egg rolls. She was surprised to see me again, but she did look better. Her hair was combed back into her usual ponytail, and her eyes weren't as swollen as they had been earlier and the bruise on her face barely showed. I think she had applied some makeup to that.

Mia ate a little food and we sat around and watched TV. Some horror flick was on. I looked at her as she was lying on the sofa. Mia looked so innocent. She was like a child trying to play grown-up games with a very grown-up man. Brice had definitely been around.

Mia and I talked for a while and I found out that we had a lot in common. I even had her laughing at one point. She was relaxed, and I actually felt relaxed myself. It was like I didn't have to be on guard with her. We were eating popcorn and getting ready to watch another horror movie when the phone rang. Mia's entire demeanor changed, and she stiffened. She asked me to answer the phone for her. It was Brice, of course. We talked for a few minutes, and I told him she was fine and what she had said earlier. He got quiet at that. Brice wanted to talk to her, but Mia wouldn't come anywhere near the phone. So finally we hung up.

I knew that the fun we were having earlier was over. Brice had totally affected Mia's mood, so I decided it was time for me to go. Before I left, I did tell Mia that she couldn't keep running from whatever was bothering her. Sooner or later she had to confront Brice, because he wouldn't be gone forever. She just looked at me with sad eyes and said she knew.

As I walked slowly down the stairs to my car, I couldn't help but think about Mia and her beautiful, sad, innocent eyes. Brice was a lucky man and didn't even know it. He took everything for granted, as though he deserved whatever he got on a silver platter. For some reason I felt frustrated and antsy, so I decided I needed a good dose of Tasha. I stopped by her apartment, and she was just what the doctor ordered.

No, I'm not a monster. Believe it or not, I'm not a horrible person. I really didn't mean to hit Mia. I don't know what happened. Hell yeah, you best believe I was mad. I was so mad I was literally seeing red, but I also meant to walk away once Mia realized I meant business. One second I was turning to walk away and the next my open hand was meeting her face. And the expression on her face when it happened, it was a look that I will never forget. First a look of surprise, then shock and then pure, pure hatred. Hatred for me.

I tried to get Mia to come out of the bathroom and listen to me. I wanted to explain, but she wouldn't leave the bathroom. She probably thought I would beat her ass some more. Mia cried most of the night—long, mournful sobs. I had to leave the next day anyway, so I decided to leave a little earlier in order to give her a chance to calm down. To be honest, I didn't have the courage to face her the next morning, to see that look of hurt and hatred in her eyes. I left and asked Christian to check in on her. I don't know what I would do without him.

I know I have to do better by Mia. She doesn't deserve all this crap I put her through, and I know she gets lonely sometimes. I know that. I thought about her all day today. It hurt me that she wouldn't come to the phone yesterday when Christian was over there. I have made a promise to myself, which I intend to keep, and that's to start treating her like the princess she is and to stop taking her for granted. When I get back home and she accepts my apology, which I know she will, I'm going to take her away for a long weekend. She'll like that, just the two of us.

If there is any consolation on my part, I did tell Mia to stay in. She was supposed to stay in and watch a movie, read or study or something. I'm not saying that she deserved what she got, but I did tell her. That's her problem. She never listens. At least maybe now she will at least listen and understand that I mean what I say.

Brice came home last night from his trip. I hadn't even talked to him since the "incident." I wasn't ready to face him yet, but Christian was right: I had to sooner or later. I had thought long and hard about what happened, and it frightened me that he could get so mad that he would hit me. I knew that Brice had a temper, but I never thought that he would put his hands on me. Boy, was I wrong.

I didn't know what time to expect him, so I ordered pizza and a Greek salad for myself. When Brice arrived I had eaten and was sitting in the living room in one of my Old Navy T-shirts watching a *New York Undercover* rerun; Malik is soooo sexy and fine with that bald head.

I heard Brice when he inserted his key in the lock and opened the door. He walked in carrying his overnight bag, and I didn't even look up. He stood in the doorway for a few minutes, unsure of what to say or do. There was this long silence. I looked up and our eyes met briefly. Amazingly, I didn't feel hate. Time had eased some of my pain, both mentally and physically. Brice spoke first.

He said, "Hi."

"Hi," I said without looking at him.

"How are you?"

"How do you think?" I asked, feeling some of my old anger resurface.

Brice slowly made his way over to near where I was still sitting on the sofa. He stopped at the recliner, faced me and stared at me for a few seconds with this apologetic look on his face.

"Listen, Mia, I'm sorry about what happened the other night. I didn't mean for things to get so out of control. You have to believe me." I still hadn't responded or even blinked an eye.

"Say something. Curse, scream, say something baby. I was so angry, and on top of that, I was drunk. Things just got out of hand. I know I said and did a lot of stupid things."

"How could you, Brice? I love you with all my heart and I would never do anything to hurt you. Why can't you trust me? You are the one who's gone all the time. How do I know you aren't screwing somebody?"

Brice stared at me as he absorbed all this.

I continued. "I trust you, Brice. I know that you love me and only me. That's why I trust you and want you to be happy and would never hurt you like you hurt me."

"Tell me what can I do to make it up to you. I'll do anything, baby. Just tell me."

"Brice, I can't tell you what to say or do. There's really nothing you can say or do at this point. The damage has been done. I will never forget you hitting me."

"Baby, at least say that you forgive me so that I can forgive myself." At that he reached down to hug me. I roughly pushed him away, because I didn't want him to touch me.

"Please, baby. I promise you that it will never happen again. I love you so much, and I don't want to ever lose you. Say that you forgive me."

I sat there and looked at him for a few seconds, wondering if he was sincere. I knew that he loved me. I really did know that much, if nothing else. But the rest of that BS . . . Would he hit me again when he let his temper get the best of him? Would he treat me better and spend more time with me? That remained to be seen.

"Brice, I forgive you, but I will not forget what you did. If you ever put your hands on me again . . . I will—and I mean it—I'll leave your ass."

I saw this sudden release in his posture, like he had been holding his breath and could exhale. "May I at least have a kiss?"

I slowly nodded my head, and Brice bent down and put his hand under my chin ever so gently and kissed me. I felt shudders go up and down my arms. I was actually trembling. It was a short, sweet kiss. He smelled and looked so good, and I had missed being in his strong arms and feeling his touch. I already felt that familiar bulge pressing against me through his pants and that familiar tingling radiating through me. For just a second I pictured how he felt deep inside of me, and I wanted him, but then I remembered his hand using my face as a punching bag.

After we pulled apart, Brice went into the bedroom to unpack, and normally I would have gone in, helped him and talked to him about his trip. But that day, I don't know, I still felt strange around him. I finally realized what it was. I was afraid of him! *Afraid of my own husband.*

14   Christian

Brice is back in town. He has been for a few days. I think he may have been avoiding me when he first got back, but we met for lunch today as we often do. He talked about everything except what was going on with him and Mia, and hey, I'm not one to pry. He has to deal with those married-people problems. I'm having enough problems of my own being a single man. Correction, being a single, black man.

I can't get Tasha off my strap. I have kicked it with her a few times at the club and at her apartment, but now I'm sick of her. She has gotten too attached. It's time to move on. I told her from the get-go, in so many words, that I was out for a good time only.

Women are all the same. They hear one thing, but think they can change us. A woman cannot change a man. Usually what you see is what you get. If he's a dog when you meet him, guess what, when you take him home he is still going to be a dog. I was straight up and honest with Tasha, but I guess she thought some good loving and good cooking would change my mind. Now she is constantly calling me and stopping by the base looking for me. Tasha really isn't that bad. I just ain't the one.

I can't deal with one woman and settling down. Sometimes I wonder how Brice does it. He went from one extreme to another, but as far as I know, and I would know, he hasn't strayed from Mia. And believe me, I know for a fact that a lot of these whores have tried. They don't care if he's married. They just want some—don't tell me that women aren't as bad as men. But Brice isn't having it.

I guess finding a good woman like Mia can reform a man. Just not this man. Mia is so sweet. When I babysat her—that's basically what I was doing—we discovered that we both love horror flicks. In fact, we watched a couple that evening. Last night, when I arrived home, I found her sitting on my stoop. Mia had bought me a horror movie classic that she wanted me to have in payment for my kindness to her. I invited her in for a few minutes.

Mia came in and looked around curiously, walking from room to room. "Now, this is truly a bachelor pad," she said as she gave me her knockout smile.

"I thought Brice was bad before I married him, but you have him beat."

"It's not that bad, is it? I thought I had it going on."

"Yes, Christian, it's bad. You have something going on, but I just don't know what," she stated.

We smiled and looked at each other the way friends do.

"So where are you headed?"

"I have to drop these books back by the library and then it's home."

We had been walking and talking and had made it to my bedroom. Mia is a trip. This girl jumped on my bed and started bouncing around.

"So this is the bed, huh? What stories it could tell."

For some reason I was embarrassed.

"Christian, I know this lady, Susan, in one of my classes would love to meet you," she said as she continued to recline on my king-sized bed.

"Mia, I don't need you to play matchmaker for me. I don't have any problems meeting women." I was gently getting her off my bed because I felt uncomfortable being in that particular room with Mia.

As I walked her back to the living room, she said, "But you haven't been meeting nice ladies. Christian, you are so sweet. You need a nice lady."

"Mia, sweet isn't something that I've been called in quite a while." I smiled. "Thanks, but no thanks."

As Mia got ready to leave, she said, "Christian, you and Brice are just alike. You think women live and die for what's between your legs. There's a lot more to most women than that."

She walked out the door and down the steps with me still looking at her with an expression of total amazement.

When I arrived back home, things were somewhat awkward for a brief period of time. Mia had reluctantly accepted my apology. I would have said and done anything for her to forgive me. I could tell that she was still hurt, though.

I had forgotten how beautiful Mia is. Whenever I'm away for a few days and return home, I always discover her beauty all over again. She had on a thin T-shirt and bikini panties when I walked through the door. Her body is so perfect. I could see the outline of her breasts and the T-shirt stopped just barely below her butt. When Mia allowed me to kiss her, it felt like heaven to hold her again. I wanted more, but I knew not to push my luck. I could feel her trembling as I held her in my arms. It was then that I realized Mia was afraid of me. I didn't know how that made me feel.

Mia still hasn't given me any yet, and I'm about to go out of my mind. She lets me sleep with her and hold her, but nothing else. This shit is messed up. I feel like a little boy on punishment. And I swear she wears stuff to bed made to torture me. Last night she had on this number that showed me what I have been missing. I was holding her close and started to fondle her breasts, and for a moment I could tell that she was aroused, but then she froze; so I stopped.

I finally received the approval for leave in order to go away for a long weekend with my wife. It's been a week since I came home, and even though Mia has forgiven me, or at least claims to, something is still missing. We are walking around each other like strangers. I don't want to do anything to upset her or frighten her and she . . . I don't know. I can't figure Mia out most of the time.

We are heading to the Blue Ridge Mountains for the weekend. I have an associate who has a cabin in the woods, and we are going to rough it. There isn't even a TV or phone, but there is a kitchen, toilet and bed. Hopefully, this weekend will put our marriage back on track. I miss Mia.

The weekend getaway was the best thing for us. When I informed Mia about my plans I saw her eyes light up again for the first time in days. Things had gotten somewhat back to normal, but we were still too polite to each other.

I went all out for our trip. I wanted everything to be perfect. I had roses delivered to the cabin, and they were waiting to greet Mia in full bloom when we arrived. I even had two large gift baskets made up for her. One was a basket of her favorites: fruit (mangos, kiwi, pineapple), chocolates (Godiva) and different flavors of tea. The other basket was filled to capacity with bubble bath, gels and lotions. There was even a bottle of champagne chilling when we stepped through the door.

Mia was like a little girl on Christmas morning; she was so excited. The cabin was nicer than I had expected; it had a rustic look, of course, and we were two miles away from the nearest neighbor. We had the woods—and each other—to ourselves. The cabin was decorated in mostly secondhand, but comfortable, furniture, which gave it a rustic charm. There was an old-fashioned stove and a fireplace stocked with firewood, and the bathroom had one of those antique, claw-foot bathtubs that sat in the center of the bathroom. Mia loved the tub. We could literally walk out our front door and be near the lake, which had our very own canoe at the water's edge.

I think I fell in love with Mia all over again. We had never had a honeymoon, which was something I had promised her, but time went by so quickly and other commitments had to be fulfilled. So this was like the honeymoon we never had, nothing glamorous or extravagant, but simple, honest and pure. I really got to know my wife as I had never known her before.

Mia and I had dated for only a month before we married, so there was a lot that I didn't know about her. But this time, with no interruptions such as TV, work or phones, we talked and got reacquainted. Mia told me her dreams and aspirations. She was going to make a great teacher. She talked about growing up, the pain she had felt when her father died and how horrible her teenage years had been with her mother being an alcoholic. She had grown up fast; my baby had been through a lot. We talked as I bathed her in the tub, we talked laying in the big solid oak bed holding each other, we talked sitting down by the lake as we had a picnic lunch and as we took nature walks hand in hand through the woods.

I even told her some things that I have never told anyone else. Things I have never even admitted to myself, let alone someone else. Mia listened and didn't pass judgment. I told her how, when I was growing up, I thought my father was jealous of me because of how Moms constantly doted on me. I was her baby and could do no wrong. I think I tried to become closer to Daddy so that he wouldn't be so jealous and take it out on Moms. Yes, I told her about the beatings Moms received and about all the women and the messing around Daddy did. Daddy was quite the ladies' man even though he had a wife and kid at home. Again, Mia didn't judge.

I proclaimed my love to her all over again. We had a mock wedding in the woods declaring our love to each other. I told her how I couldn't live without her and how when she came into my life everything had changed for the better. I didn't want to sleep around and be "out there." I told her that she was my heart and soul. We made love that night for the first time in ages. It was slow, gentle and tender. I wanted to show her what my heart felt and couldn't put into words. When it was over and she lay on top of me, skin to skin, I could feel her heartbeat pounding away and I felt totally at peace because I knew she was the one. I had found my soul mate.

We returned to the base ready to resume our married life and be a happily married couple again. So much had been said and so many promises made. *We were ready to begin again.*

That wonderful weekend that Brice and I spent in the Blue Ridge Mountains of North Carolina was a godsend. It completely rejuvenated our tense marriage. I mean, it is over a year later and we are still together. Don't get me wrong. Things didn't change overnight, but Brice was willing to try, and so was I. That made all the difference in the world. We both realized that there was so much that we didn't know about each other. After all, we had dated only one month before we tied the knot. I felt like I knew and understood him better after that weekend.

We arrived back at the base like true honeymooners, with eyes only for each other. The past year has flown by so fast. I'm almost twenty-four years old, but I feel so much older. Being married has made me grow up. I'm still working towards that dream of obtaining my degree, and I'm almost there. Brice is still recruiting all over the place; the Marines are always looking for a few good men.

Oh, and let's not forget Christian. He is constantly around our apartment. He drops by whenever he wants to, and that's fine with me. He eats, showers and sometimes even sleeps over. Christian never did take me up on my offer to find a nice lady for him. From the bits and pieces of conversation that I pick up from him and Brice, he's still running around being as whorish as ever. Brice is always telling me to mind my own business; Christian is a big boy and can take care of himself. I look at Christian sometimes and see such sadness. I just want him to be happy.

Yeah, life was good again. We were living our peaceful, routine, married life with only a few episodes of drama tossed in here and there. Nothing major. Just a few disagreements, but with nothing physical besides our lovemaking, which was still going as strong and as sweet as ever.

One Friday evening I received a phone call from Mama; we usually spoke every Sunday afternoon, and she would catch me up on what was going on back home. So I knew something was wrong the minute I answered the phone and heard her muffled voice.

"Mama, what's wrong?" I asked right away.

"Mia, it's your uncle Larry," she said.

"What is it, Mama?"

"Baby, he had a massive heart attack about three hours ago, and they don't know if he is going to make it. Can you and Brice make it home?"

"Brice is out of town this weekend. Don't worry. I'll get there, though."

"Okay, baby. Let me give you the number at the hospital. Try to get here as soon as possible. And say a prayer for your uncle."

"Bye, Mama. I'll see you soon."

I hung up the phone with the start of fresh tears and immediately called Christian. After telling him of my predicament, he volunteered to drive me to Georgia and make arrangements for Brice to be contacted to meet us there. That way we could leave right away, as soon as we packed some overnight bags. We could get there by early morning.

Once we had fueled up and hit the interstate, the tears started flowing freely again. I didn't want to cry in front of Christian, but every time I thought of losing my favorite uncle, I couldn't contain myself. Uncle Larry reminded me of my daddy so much because they looked alike, but also because he had this easygoing, laid-back manner.

I could tell that the crying made Christian a bit uncomfortable. He was driving and trying to console me by saying that everything would be okay; Uncle Larry would be fine. He tried to get me to laugh and talk, but I wasn't up to that. I finally was all cried out, so

I curled up over by the passenger door and tried to nap for a while. Christian had turned the radio to some golden oldies station as we drove into Georgia. It was raining most of the way, which made me think of that song "A Rainy Night in Georgia." We drove in a comfortable silence while the sounds of soft music filled the air with only my occasional sobs.

I must have finally dozed off because I awoke to find Christian sitting beside me in the car, staring at me as I slept.

He said, "Do you have to use the restroom, or can I get you some coffee?"

"No, no thanks. I'm fine. Where are we?" I asked as I sat up and stretched.

Christian said, "We have about another hour and a half before we reach Atlanta."

"God, how long have I been asleep? You should have woken me and had me drive some. I know you're tired."

"No, I'm cool. Driving has always relaxed me, and you were knocked out. You look so peaceful when you sleep. Like an angel."

I laughed and said, "An angel with drool and all."

He looked at me for a few moments as if there was something more that needed to be said. I lowered my eyes first, and Christian got out of the car to finish gassing up. After our pit stop, I was fully awake, and I was determined not to start crying all over again. Uncle Larry was going to be all right. He was strong with the will to live. So as we rode into the early morning and watched the sun rise from Christian's car, I talked and talked and talked about my uncle Larry.

Right before we arrived at the hospital, I thanked Christian wholeheartedly for being there for me. He said that he would do anything for me because that's what friends are for.

As soon as we arrived on the eighth floor of the critical-care unit and went into the sterile waiting room looking for Mama and my other relatives, I spotted Mama over in the corner and I knew that we were too late. Uncle Larry had died only thirty minutes earlier. I don't remember much from that point other than Christian holding me in his muscular arms, rubbing my back and telling me over and over that everything was going to be all right. He said that he would take care of me and everything was going to be all right. With those soothing words whispered in my ear, I believed him. It felt strange being in another man's arms, but with Christian I felt safe and secure.

Time stood still. It seemed like I sat in that sterile, cold waiting room consoling and holding Mia for hours. She was quite upset, as were other members of her family. Uncle Larry was loved, that was obvious. I think Mia had convinced herself that he was going to make it. I found out later that he had suffered a milder heart attack a few years earlier. Some people can never change old habits to healthier ones. I sat there and rocked and rocked and rocked Mia until her crying subsided.

Everyone started getting up in a daze and making plans. Somebody finally got her uncle Larry's widow, Aunt Ruth, to a car and home. We were meeting back over at her house. They decided that the funeral would be Monday, so they had to make most of the arrangements that Saturday, since the next day would be Sunday and businesses would be closed.

Mia and I volunteered to make most of the phone calls to loved ones to give them the sad news and to do some of the running around for the older people. Mia was great; once she composed herself, she was up and running—ready to help out any way she could. And I was more than willing to assist. I made some phone calls and finally got in touch with Brice's superior and left an urgent message for him to call.

Mia and I were back at her aunt Ruth's house, sitting around as friends, relatives and acquaintances were constantly in and out, bringing food and their condolences. There was food everywhere you looked, and we had tried to get Ruth to eat, but she wouldn't touch a thing. She kept crying for Larry to come back to her. They had been married for almost forty years.

This was bringing up so many memories that I thought I had forgotten or had at least tried to forget. This reminded me so much of when my Moms died. The food, the people, the looks of sympathy in my direction, the crying . . . This was too much. I had to get out of there and get a breath of fresh air. I had gone to the coatrack to retrieve my blue down jacket when Mia came around the corner.

She asked, "Are you going out?"

"Yeah, I need to get some fresh air. I was going to ride out if you don't need anything."

"Do you mind if I come along? I need a break. We finally got Aunt Ruth to eat something, but I feel like I'm going to break down any minute. Christian, I loved him so much," she said, close to tears again.

"Come on. Let's get out of here for a while," I said as I gently took her hand.

Mia grabbed her jacket, and we headed out the door. We drove around for a little while, not really going anywhere in particular, just lost in our own separate thoughts. The town had changed so much over the years. Mia and I ended up over at Carver Homes, my former home in the projects.

I don't know why I even went there. When I was in town, I usually avoided that area like the plague because it held too many memories. Memories that I had long ago suppressed. But today, I don't know . . . today made those memories resurface.

I parked the car and told Mia, "Let's walk for a while."

She nodded, and I went around and opened the door for her.

"I used to live here in that brick building on the third floor. You see, the one over in the corner at the end of the hallway," I said as I pointed it out for her.

"Brice told me what happened to your mother. That must have been devastating with you being so young."

"Yeah, I guess it was, but shit happens. You have to deal with what life throws your way. Brice's family took me in and made me feel like family, like I belonged somewhere."

We walked some more in silence. The neighborhood was even more rundown than I remembered. Beer bottles, cigarettes and the smell of reefer was in the air as little kids ran around dirty, shoeless and unchaperoned. Nothing had changed.

Mia said, as if sensing my mood, "Well, one good thing came out of here: you."

Later, we were back at her aunt Ruth's, and even more people had arrived, if that were possible. Everybody had a story to tell about Larry that had us all laughing. He must have been a good man. Mia, I don't know where she was, somewhere trying to take care of someone. Brice had called earlier and said he would make it into town on Sunday on Delta Air Lines. As I watched Mia talking to him, I noticed her almond-shaped eyes light up and she was even laughing a little. Mia hung up with, "I love you, baby."

I must have dozed off on the sofa because I awoke to someone making a lot of racket with this loud laugh.

"Oh, no, it can't be. Oh my God."

When I opened my eyes to see who was making all the noise, it was Reggie, Brice's cousin. I hadn't seen that man in years.

"Hey, what's up, man?" I asked as we shook hands.

"You know a little this, a little that. I thought that was you. So where is your partner?"

I explained that Brice would arrive the next day and that I had driven Mia down.

"How are they doing, man? I still can't believe that that sweet little thing married that dog," he said jokingly.

"Fine, I guess. Mia is around here somewhere."

Reggie finally stumbled off down the hallway. It looked like he had had a few too many beers. He said that he would check with me later. Yeah, Reggie and I went a ways back. I dated his sister for a minute when we were in high school. That chick was crazy about me. I had heard that she was married now with four or five kids.

I laid my head back against the sofa again and people-watched for a while. I spotted Mia over in the corner talking to some lady dressed from head to toe in black. She was taking this grieving thing to the extreme. I talked with Gloria, Reggie's wife, for a few minutes also. She said that things were going all right for them, but Reggie still loved to drink a little too much.

I was still sitting in my spot on the sofa and was alone at last. Mia had brought me a plate earlier, but I didn't really have an appetite. I saw Reggie headed back in my direction more intoxicated than ever.

"My man, my man. You still sitting over here? You should have come out back and gotten yourself a brew," he said.

"No man, I'm fine."

Reggie was standing there, peering down at me with this stupid look and a grin on his face. Just grinning.

"What's up?" I asked.

"Nothing, you and Brice are a trip, that's all."

I looked at him with a confused expression on my face. I was really trying hard to follow him and figure out what the hell he was talking about.

"You really blew it, man, with sis."

"Reggie," I asked, "do you know how long ago that was? We were children."

"I know, but you hurt her, man. She loved you, and you stepped all over her heart. No you stumped all over her heart. She would have done anything for you, and how did you repay her? You fucked her and dumped her."

"Man, that's water under the bridge."

"Not for her. Not for me it isn't," he said.

I looked at this drunken fool talking about stuff that had happened over twelve years ago like it happened yesterday. Yeah, I fucked his sister. Who didn't? She got what she wanted in the backseat of my car a few times.

"You and Brice used to think y'all owned all the pussy in town. I'm not playa hating now, but shit, man, don't y'all care about anybody? Brice, Brice was just cold-blooded with women, but I thought you were a little different. Just a little different."

"Reggie, what right do you have to try to tell me how to live or to place judgment on me? Get out of my damn face until you sober up and can talk with some damn sense."

"No, man, you hear me out first."

Reggie was starting to get loud, so I decided to listen for a few more minutes.

"Okay. Okay."

"Sis never got over you or the abortion."

My face must have registered much shock and surprise, because he gave me a look of smug satisfaction that he had finally broken through and gotten to me.

"You didn't know, did you? Yeah, she was pregnant and had an abortion. She told Mama that it was yours, but she knew you wouldn't want it. You had just left for the military. So she got rid of it."

"You know she has four boys, living down in Alabama. She even named one of them after you. But payback is a bitch, ain't it?"

"What are you talking about now?" I asked as I recovered from the shock of what he had just told me.

"Man, I can see how Mia has your nose wide open. You are in love with her; it shows all over your face. You and Brice really do share and share alike, huh?"

"Man, get the fuck out of my face."

"Okay, but I can tell. You are in love, probably for the first time in your life, and she doesn't want you. Every time she walks into the room your eyes light up. I've been watching, man."

"Yeah, my man is in love with his best friend's wife. Ain't that some shit? Yeah, payback is a bitch," he repeated as he stumbled off, laughing.

That muthafucka. I would have kicked his ass if we hadn't been in Mia's aunt Ruth's house. I didn't want to disrespect her like that. All that bullshit he was talking. Reggie could be a mean muthafucka once he got a little liquor in him. I could care less about that sister of his . . . Like I said, she'd gotten what she wanted . . . several times.

But that shit about Mia. I love Mia . . . just like a sister and would do anything for her.

Mia chose that moment to walk back over to check on me.

I said, "Look, Mia, I'm going to go out for a while to visit a few people." I had a certain female in mind, but I didn't tell her that.

Mia looked at me for a moment. "Are you all right?"

"Yeah, I'm fine," I said as I spotted Reggie watching us from the corner with an obvious smirk on his drunken face.

"Look, I'll see you later," I said as I made my way to the front door.

We were to stay over at Mia's mother's house. She had already given me a spare key to her house. I got back late that night and tried my best to be quiet as I made my way up the stairs to the bedroom where my overnight bag lay. Everyone was asleep. I didn't see Mia and the TV was off. I didn't want anyone to see me either; I looked like a wild man. My eyes were bloodshot because the drive and the day's events had finally caught up with me. And . . . Meshell, whose house I had just left, had tried to wear me out. She couldn't get enough.

I located the bedroom at the end of the hallway, went in and somehow managed to change into my pajama bottoms. I did remember to at least pack those. At home I usually slept in my Calvin's. I was asleep before my head hit the pillow.

The next morning I probably would have slept the day away, but I was awakened by a gentle, timid knock at my door. It was Mia. I had propped myself up on two elbows and still had the sheet wrapped around me when Mia stuck her head in and asked if she could come in. I nodded.

"Hi, sleepyhead," she said as she entered slowly and came over to sit by me on the bed.

"Hi," I said. This girl always made me feel uneasy when we were alone. I didn't know if I should cover up my exposed upper body or not.

"I wanted to let you know that breakfast is ready," she said.

If she was uncomfortable with me being half naked, she didn't show it.

"Listen, Christian, I wanted to say thank you for all you have done for me. I couldn't have gotten through all this without you." She then leaned over and gave me a quick kiss on the cheek.

"Mia, I would do anything for you. You know that. You are a good friend, just like Brice."

Mia sat there as though she were letting this sink in for a while. Then I saw her staring at my bare chest.

"Where did you get that? That is sooo beautiful."

She was referring to a gold cross that I always wore around my neck.

"That is really beautiful," she said again as she gently lifted it up to get a better look. As she placed it back on my chest, her finger lingered there for a few seconds and I felt chills.

I coughed. "Huh, it belonged to my Moms. She wore it to church every Sunday. So when she passed, I received it. I wear it all the time. It never comes off."

"Well, I had better help Mama set the table. Come down when you're ready."

After she had left and closed the door, I slowly laid back down. Not one lady I had slept with had ever even asked about my cross. Never. And I had slept with many. But Mia noticed.

I finally made it downstairs, after showering and dressing in jeans, sneakers and sweatshirt, and I had a delicious breakfast of grits, eggs, bacon, sausage, pancakes and orange juice and coffee. I hadn't realized I was so hungry.

The remainder of the morning was spent back over at Mia's aunt Ruth's. Finally, at around one o'clock, Brice arrived. He looked like he had been through hell and back. He had a day-old beard and bloodshot eyes. Brice looked horrible. As soon as Mia saw him, she ran into his arms. He held her and told her how sorry he was. We spoke and talked for a while, but for the rest of the evening they were inseparable.

That night we half watched a football game on TV at Mia's house and basically crashed. The funeral was the next day, so everyone retired to bed rather early. We were all emotionally and physically drained by then anyway. I was the last to hit the sack because I felt restless and nervous for some reason. I turned off the TV about an hour after everyone else had gone up to bed. I lay in bed in the bedroom that Mia used to sleep in as a little girl and thought. Thought about my life up until that point in time.

Brice and Mia were next door in the guest bedroom because it was larger. I had lain in bed for what seemed like hours. The house was in total darkness and complete silence. Suddenly, I heard Mia crying softly in the stillness of the night. Evidently their bed faced the wall of the bed that I slept in. As I listened closer, I realized Mia wasn't crying, but that what I heard were cries of ecstasy. I heard Mia softly moaning as Brice made love to her. I guess they were trying to be quiet, but the house was quiet and sound traveled. The sounds got louder and more urgent.

I heard Brice whispering something to her. I heard Mia calling out his name. And then more moaning and groaning. I fell asleep with images of Mia opening her silky legs to be entered and the cries of unborn babies. Babies that called me Daddy.

I still can't believe that Uncle Larry is gone. He was always my sunshine on a rainy day. After Daddy died, he was there for me and Mama and was a constant reminder of Daddy to me, since they looked so much alike and had that same fun-loving, compassionate nature. So many people tell me that I'm just like them; I take that as a compliment.

Uncle Larry once told me that Daddy would be so proud of me and what I'm doing with my life. He was always making me feel good about myself and my accomplishments, such as graduating with honors from Booker T. Washington High School and being accepted into college on scholarship.

To be honest, he wasn't that thrilled about my quick marriage to Brice. Uncle Larry thought I was too young to marry. I still remember that conversation as if it took place yesterday. I was sitting on the sofa at Mama's house, drinking a soda and watching *Ricki Lake* when Uncle Larry dropped by. I heard him and Mama in the kitchen whispering, so I was sure I was the topic of that whispered conversation. I continued to watch *Ricki Lake*. Uncle Larry finally appeared around the corner dressed in his usual khaki pants, workshirt, cap and a big smile just for me.

"Hey, sweetpea"—that was a nickname that had stuck with me since birth—"what's this I hear about you getting married on me?"

I turned away from the show, whose topic of the day was Men Who Control Their Women Too Much, and gave Uncle Larry my full attention.

"Mama couldn't wait to call and tell you, could she?"

"Ahhh now, sweetpea, don't be like that. You know your mama is only looking out for your well-being, and you should have been the one calling me."

I just looked at him for a second and then smiled. I couldn't be upset with him. Uncle Larry was my favorite uncle.

"Well . . .?"

"It's true. I met this Marine, Brice Matthew," I said as a faint smile crept across my face from just thinking about him. "I love him so much, Uncle Larry, and we are getting married in a few days."

"Were you planning on informing your dear old uncle of this major event in your life?"

I just shrugged and looked away.

"Baby, what's the rush? You don't really know this man, and he is eight years older than you."

"I love him and I know all I need to know. I see Mama didn't leave out any of the details."

Uncle Larry took his cap off and sat down on the love seat directly across from me.

"Mia, we are just concerned about you, that's all. We don't want you to rush into anything that you'll regret later. You are known to leap first and look later."

"Uncle Larry, you don't understand. I love Brice so much. For the longest time, I have been looking for someone who could complete me and make me whole. I just know that he is my soul mate in life. We were meant to be together. We have so much in common, and he treats me so special. I feel like a queen when I'm with him. And age, age is nothing but a number. I have never felt anything like this with the boys I dated in the past."

He sat there silently, gave me his undivided attention and stared intensely at me as I went on and on about Brice, the man of my dreams. I was trying my best to convince him that this marriage would work and was not a mistake. I wanted, no needed, his approval probably more than Mama's.

He finally scratched his head and said, "I see you've put a lot of thought into this. You aren't jumping in blindly. I don't know about all of this destiny, fate stuff, but you have always been the romantic. Marriage is hard work, Mia. It's not a game, and it's not about playing house. It's not something you can step into lightly. You take your vows seriously. It's for better or for worse. And sometimes there may be more worse than better. Matthew . . . I vaguely remember or have heard of that family. They live over on Washington Street, don't they?"

I nodded my head.

"Mia, I know your mama and me would like to keep you as an innocent child for as long as we can and shield you from the cruel world. Lord knows, you have seen and been through enough already. Sometimes I forget that you have grown into a beautiful, intelligent, loving young woman right before my eyes. Girl, I remember when you were knee high to a tadpole, running around in diapers, sucking on a pacifier. Your father would be so proud of you, but I know that he is looking down on you and he's proud.

"I can't tell you what to do or what not to do. You're grown, but I'm not going to lie. I wish you would give this marriage thing some time. What's the rush? If you love him so much and he loves you so much, then that love will still be there six months, a year from now. Get to know each other a little better first."

"We don't want to wait. I don't want anyone else and neither does he. We know this is right."

"Okay. You are headstrong just like me, so I can't be mad. You're going to do exactly what you want to anyhow. If he makes you happy, you tell this Brice that we welcome him into the family and he better not hurt my sweetpea in any way, form or fashion. You hear me?"

"Yes, sir, I hear you." We both smiled, and Uncle Larry stood up to give me a big hug and a kiss on the cheek.

"I love you, baby. You bring Brice by the house and let me meet the man who has stolen my baby girl away."

"Okay, I'll do that. But he hasn't stolen me away. I'll always be your sweetpea, no matter what."

"I guess you'll be moving to North Carolina, then."

"Yes, but don't worry about school. I'll just transfer to a university there. I am going to graduate with my bachelor's degree in education. Don't worry about that."

"You better! Mia, I give you my blessing. Brice is a lucky man, and I hope he knows that."

That was that. After Uncle Larry gave us his blessing, Mama finally came around too. She really valued his opinion and respected him. Plans were finalized, Uncle Larry gave me away with a big smile on his face and tears in his eyes, and Brice and I were married. When the preacher pronounced us man and wife, I was the happiest lady in the world because I had searched high and low to find the one for me and I thought I had found my black knight.

We left for North Carolina right after the funeral. I really hated to leave Mama and everyone behind. So many relatives and friends came out to the funeral service because Uncle Larry had so many people who loved him. I still can't get over how Brice and Christian were supportive. I couldn't have gotten through this without them, especially Christian.

Christian never ceases to amaze me. Christian and Brice are alike in many ways, yet Christian has this tender, compassionate side that he keeps hidden. I'm not a psychiatrist or anything, but I feel that he never got over the death of his mother. I mean, he wears this beautiful cross next to his heart that belonged to his mother, which he hasn't taken off since the day she died.

Yes, Brice and Christian have quite a rare bond and commitment to each other. I think it is wonderful, great, for two black men to have a strong bond. In this day and age, an unconditional love for each other is uplifting. Sometimes I think they can read each other's minds; I know they can finish each other's sentences. Brice would do anything for Christian, and vice versa. Actually, I sorta envy their relationship. I don't have a girlfriend or cousin or anyone who is that close to me.

But getting back to Christian. He was unbelievable. He drove me to Atlanta and did whatever was needed once we got there. I never heard him complain, not even once. I have to do something special for him now that we are back, maybe cook dinner for him or buy him a CD. Well, probably not cook. Brice has him thinking that I'm the worst cook in the world. Christian would probably be afraid to eat anything I made. Brice was there for me as well, but sometimes I feel that his job comes before me.

Christian is so fine and he doesn't even know it. Ummmm. He should find himself someone nice and settle down like me and Brice. I had gone into his room, my old bedroom, where he was sleeping, to thank him for everything when we were still in Georgia, and I woke him up. The brotha was fine. When I came in he was propped up in bed showing off that broad, muscle-toned, flat-as-an-ironing-board stomach of his. He was lying back with his legs spread open with only a thin sheet partially covering him from the waist down, and he had this sexy, sleepy look in his eyes. I thought at that moment, *Damn, just rub a little oil on him and he could be this month's* Playgirl *centerfold.* Yeah, the brotha is definitely fine. I could only imagine what was underneath the sheet.

I just know he heard me and Brice making love the night before the funeral. I told Brice that the walls were too thin, and I knew that Christian's bed was against the same wall as our bed, but you know Brice. He never takes no for an answer. He said that we would be quiet, but once he started laying it on me with all he had, it was hard to remain quiet. Brice was doing it so good, and it was feeling so good, that for a second I forgot where I was. So I know that Christian heard, and the next morning I felt embarrassed when he said good morning to us. He gave me this smile like "I know what you did last night." Maybe he didn't hear, but I think he did. Brice didn't care. When I mentioned it to him that Christian might have heard, he just laughed and said he got an earful. I swear, sometimes Brice pisses me off so much. I know that it's bad to say, but he probably wanted him to hear me moan and groan. "Check this out, man. Listen to how I can make my wife beg for it. Listen to her moan as I stick it to her. She can't get enough of this dick."

I had all kinds of crazy dreams that night. My last dream, the one that woke me up, was of Christian and me making love. It was so real. I guess I was tired from the previous events and worried about him hearing us that I dreamed Christian had me in his strong arms, making tender, sweet love to me. It's amazing what a combination of stress and lack of sleep can do.

On the drive back home, they let me sit in the backseat so that I could get some much-needed sleep. They took turns driving. I sat back there and thought for quite a while about my life. Funerals can do that to us; make us think about our own immortality. I listened and observed the only two men in my life. They were so much alike, yet so different. They were like two little boys, laughing and talking as we drove the long road back to North Carolina. I fell asleep shortly after I heard Brice tell Christian that some lady named Tasha had been on base trying to track him down. Brice joked that Christian must have really whipped it on her. Christian laughed at that and asked, "What do you think?" When I woke up again, we were almost home.

If only I had known that the next few months would be like walking on eggshells, I probably would have stayed in Georgia with my mother. Brice was seriously tripping again and taking it out on me. My husband is very competitive. He always has to be the best or he thinks he's a failure.

I can't do anything right, let him tell it. Lately, he always has me near tears or crying. Our lovemaking isn't tender and gentle anymore. It has gotten to the point where I don't want Brice to touch me because he is always too forceful and aggressive during sex. It's like he's taking his anger out on my stuff, and if I protest that just makes it worse for me. Even foreplay, something as simple as touching my breasts, is torture. He will squeeze, pinch, bite, grope and cause me just enough pain to make me pull away. So I cry and try to get him off me, and Brice just pushes me back down, grabs my ass, spreads my legs and plunges it in, all of it, and tells me I am his wife so I had better learn to perform my wifely duties.

Christian knows something is going on, because he is constantly asking me if I'm all right. He says that I look sad sometimes. I tell him that I'm fine, but I need to take care of myself, eat properly and stop burning the candle on both ends. He thinks that school is taking its toll on me. What am I supposed to tell him? "Your best friend is making my life a living hell. He abuses me with his dick." If only he knew. Maybe he does know—they tell each other everything. School is my salvation. It takes me away from the apartment, gets me around people my age and is a welcome distraction.

In time . . . this all passed and Brice was once again my wonderful husband, treating me like a princess and making plans for our Christmas vacation.

19 Christian

Time flies when you're having fun . . . Yeah, right. It's almost Christmas again. The malls are already packed to capacity and bustling with shoppers ready to shell out their hard-earned money on some gift that will be shoved into the back of somebody's closet. Everybody is festive and in good cheer. Give me a break. The children are on their best behavior so that Santa will pay them a visit, and the mistletoe has been hung. Merry Christmas. The true meaning has been lost somewhere. When Moms was alive she made sure I understood the true meaning. She loved Christmas so much.

I don't know what I'll do this year. Years past I have gone home with Brice to visit his parents, but I think I'll be a third wheel this year, with Mia and all. I guess I'll hang out here and get some rest. I finally got Tasha, much to her displeasure, off my back, and I'm just hanging loose for a while. To get rid of Tasha, I had to completely be a dog and break it down to her, but I have found that some women don't understand it any other way. The way I broke it down to her, she couldn't help but get my point. I know that's brutal, but it's a fact. I'm taking a much-needed break from women.

Speaking of Mia and Brice, I think they need some time away. Whenever I go over there, there is always tension in the air. Sometimes I think Mia is afraid of him. I feel sorry for her because Brice is always riding her about something. Lately it's her cooking. When he walks through the door, dinner has to be on the table. I was having dinner with them the other evening and he literally had her in tears because the chicken was too tough. Mia was sitting at the table, trying her best to hold back the tears, but Brice was relentless. He kept riding her until she broke down. When she ran out of the room, he kept right on talking like nothing had happened. I love the man, but Brice can be a mean son of a bitch sometimes. He can be cold. I mean, that's not some hoochie that he picked up on the street. That's his wife he's dogging like that.

Hey, but what can I say? Absolutely nothing. He is the one married to her. I can't interfere in my man's affairs. He wears the pants in that household. But now, if it were me, I would treat Mia with respect. He still doesn't realize how lucky he is. Brice is spoiled. Always has been. His Moms did that, and he has always thought he deserved everything he received like it was his right or something.

The girl loves the man. She must, to put up with all his bullshit. Don't get me wrong—Brice is my partner—but wrong is wrong. Did I say that? I think a little bit of Mia is starting to rub off on me.

I know Mia was all excited because they were going home for Christmas. She's like a little girl sometimes. They are going to stay at Brice's parents. She was asking me what I thought he wanted for a Christmas gift and then she surprised me by asking me what I wanted. Mia said, "Christian, I love you like a brother. I have to get you something really special as well. I consider you my friend too, not just Brice's." I told her anything she chose would be great. She just smiled secretly.

You don't have to tell me . . . I know that I've been a total ass, to put it mildly, for the last few months. Ever since we returned after Mia's uncle's funeral, I have been this way. When I should have been supportive and comforting Mia, I was doing the opposite. But I couldn't help myself. It was like that line Flip Wilson made famous in the early seventies . . . *"The devil made me do it."*

I know that's a sorry excuse, but when I'm unhappy or stressed it's like I don't want anyone else to be happy, either. Since things were not going my way at work, I treated Mia like shit for two months. I don't know why she hasn't left my ass by now. I don't deserve her; I know that. Yet she still loves me and tries so hard to make things right and be the good little wife.

Such simple things please my wife. When I told her that we were going home for Christmas break, she was ecstatic. We need to get away and just chill. Mia will be on Christmas break from her studies, and I need a few days myself. We saw the folks briefly when we were home last time, but our main focus was on Mia's family. Moms can't wait to see us, and I'm sure she will put some meat on Mia's frame and bug her about having some grandchildren before she is too old to enjoy them.

I tried to talk Christian into coming also, but he said that he would be a third wheel. He knows Moms and Daddy love him like a son, but he thinks he will interfere with me and Mia. I don't know what's going on with him lately. I don't understand him. He told me that he is going to cool it with the "dating game" for a while.

I asked, "So what exactly does that mean—you're going to cool it?"

Christian responded, "Man, I'm sick of playing the game. I'm burnt out. I wanna chill for a minute. Get my head together. Is anything wrong with that?"

I shook my head, but still didn't know where he was coming from, so I asked, "What brought all this on?"

"I don't know. Man, I'm thirty-one, almost thirty-two years old and still out there with my main purpose being to have fun and get some pussy. There has to be more to life than that." He laughed. "Maybe I'll meet a nice lady and settle down, like you, and have a couple of rug rats who look just like their old man."

"No, my man ain't talking about settling down. Not you."

"Well, things change. I've changed. I don't know man . . . there has to be more to life."

"Well, just do what you have to do. I got your back."

I can't put my finger on it, but something is definitely bugging Christian. I have known him too long not to know that something is up. He can be so secretive at times, but in time, like always, he will let me know what's up when he's ready.

I am seriously thinking about starting our family. Mia is almost through with getting her degree, and now would be the perfect time to bring a baby into our family circle. She can take a few years off to raise our son before starting her teaching career. I know it will be a son because real men produce sons. We didn't discuss children before we married, but there were a lot of things that we didn't discuss. I have always wanted two boys to carry on the family name. Mia, I'm sure she wants a little girl to dress up and spoil. Regardless, though, I think it's time. Mia is always telling me how bored she is because she doesn't do anything but go to school and come home. A baby will keep her occupied. Daddy used to joke that the best way to keep a woman was barefoot and pregnant. It's ironic that they could have only one child—me. If Moms were capable, I may have had a house full of brothers and sisters.

We leave for Georgia in a few days. Maybe I'll bring up the pregnancy issue at that time. Who knows, maybe we will begin our family in Georgia.

I should have known that everything was going too perfectly. Lately, nothing seems to work out for me. We were packed, excited and ready to begin our vacation, but the Marines want to own a black man. My man anyway. They called, and Brice is on some trip . . . Translation, he will meet me in Georgia at his parents' house once he has finished. I was so pissed. Brice was like, "Damn, get over it, baby. You don't complain when the Marines pay the bills, put food on the table or pay for your education."

We were finally getting along again and now this. We desperately needed this time away together. Brice kept reminding me that he would be away only a few days. I told him that I would stay at home with my mama until he arrived, but he stated that his Moms was expecting us and he wanted me there. Brice always wants something from me but is never willing to give anything back in return. I am so sick of his shit. I really am.

As much as I hate to admit it, I realize, Brice controls me and everything about me. He controls when I eat, where I go, how I dress, when we screw, how we screw and on and on and on. He probably thinks I would stop breathing if he told me to. He informed me the other day that I needed to gain a few pounds because I was getting too skinny. Brice said that he liked a woman with some meat on her bones. I started to tell him that I wouldn't have lost weight if he weren't driving me out of my damn mind. But no, I just left it alone in order to maintain the peace. Also, I find that I curse more and more, and Brice can curse like a soldier, excuse the pun, but he can't stand it if I curse.

Did I tell you that when he is out of town on a trip, he calls me every night to check on me, not to say hello, but to check on me? I have to be in and answer his call. I can't go out with anyone other than Christian. I've accepted the fact that Christian is my babysitter. I know he comes over all the time to watch me, but he's cool. Actually, we have a lot in common and he always has me laughing. We watch horror movies, quote the lines before they even say them, eat ice cream out of the same container and have a great time.

One time Brice called while I was still at the library studying, and he almost had a fit. After that he started accusing me of screwing around on him. Brice went on and on so that I finally had to hang up on him. He kept calling back, cursing and shouting, until I eventually unplugged the phone. When he arrived home, he didn't mention his behavior or apologize. After that, Christian, my sitter, was around even more.

I know. I know. I'm sounding and acting like a complete fool. Any other strong, black female—and I am a strong, black female—would have set him straight or left his ass by now. Don't you think I know that? But I love him. I know it sounds so corny and so typical, but I do. Deep down, under all of his macho shit, Brice is a good man, and regardless of all the shit he puts me through, he loves me. I know he hasn't screwed anyone else, he provides for us, he takes care of me, and when he makes love to me, if he isn't upset, he makes me feel like the most loved woman in the world. So I think that I can put up with his mess. Anyway, he acts stupid only when he's stressed out about something or other. He just got his much-wanted and well-deserved promotion, so he'll be happy for a while. When he's happy, I'm happy. That's the problem with so many marriages. At the first sign of trouble, the parties are in divorce court. No one tries to work things out anymore. Well, I took my vows seriously. For better or for worse.

I'm not some stupid, uneducated sister who is going to stand by and let her man beat her down to the ground or under the ground.

I love him, but I am not going to love him to death. Right now, we are still getting used to each other.

I drove down to Georgia yesterday and my mother-in-law, Vivica, has made things pleasant enough for me. She is such a kind, gentle lady. I really like and admire her. Her only annoying habit is asking me about grandchildren all the time. I am not ready for children yet; someday, but not this day. I haven't even started my career yet. I would love to have a beautiful daughter to spoil and love, and of course she would be the spitting image of me. And Brice isn't ready either. Right now, I'm his baby.

The night before I left for Georgia, he was ever so gentle in our lovemaking. He knew I was still pissed. The man knows how to make me feel soooo good when he wants to though. Brice is not a selfish lover like some men; he wants me to get mine too. In fact, I think he enjoys seeing me come just as much as he likes coming. It proves to him that he is a real man when I am squirming and moaning underneath him. Brice has such an ego that has to be stroked. No, needs to be stroked. I will stroke that ego any day if he continues to stroke my body like he did the other night. And we did it on the bathroom counter again before I walked out the door for my long trip. He was stroking me long and deep from behind, rubbing my breasts and whispering for me not to see any of my old boyfriends once I hit town. I was like, "Okay, baby. Anything you say. Just don't stop what you are doing . . . It feels so good."

Guess who showed up last night? Christian. He said that he changed his mind about spending a lonely Christmas on base. I know that Brice called him and asked him to come. Sometimes I wonder what hold Brice has over Christian. I guess they are just good friends.

I was so happy to see him. Lately he has been different. I can't explain how, but something is different about him. Sometimes when he is over and we are watching TV or talking, I'll see something in his eyes, or sometimes I will turn to say something to him and catch him staring at me, and he will turn away as if I have caught him at something.

Christian and I talk about all sorts of things. He is like the big brother that I never had. We can talk about everything and anything and I don't feel embarrassed. One night, we were watching this very steamy, sexy flick, on HBO, and I could tell that it was turning him on. So I playfully asked, "Christian, how do you like to make love? What's your technique?"

Christian looked at me like I was retarded or close to it. "Mia, what kind of question is that?"

"Christian, what don't you understand about it? HOW-DO-YOU-MAKE-LOVE?"

I could see the beginnings of a smile forming on his lips as he looked at me and said, "Mia, you better stop all that flirting that you do so well; it's going to get your ass in trouble one day. You're going to get something or someone you can't handle. I know Brice doesn't—"

"Christian, Brice doesn't own me. I am only married to him. Educate me. I want to know what you like. You can ask me anything too, and I'll answer. Okay?"

"Why do you want to know what I like? Are you going to do something for me?"

"No, but I can pass the info on to Susan."

"You don't give up, do you? I told you that I'm not interested in Susan," he said with a smile.

"Well . . . ?"

"Well, what?"

"Tell me."

Christian looked at me for a moment and then he went on to describe in graphic detail how he liked oral sex and what he would do to his lover and what he liked for his partner to do to him. By the time he was finished, I was extremely embarrassed, and I blushed like a virgin.

That was one thing that Brice wasn't into, at least not on the giving end. He would try to push my head down there in a minute. Usually, I would just kiss around it, below it, to the side of it, kiss it and move on, but one night he was pissed at me about something. I can't remember what because he was always pissed at me about something or other. Oh, he thought I had flirted with this salesman at the mall, at the cosmetics counter. Anyway, Brice was determined that I was going to "go downtown," as my punishment, I guess. He knew I didn't like doing that, not even for him. He wouldn't relent until I did it. My tears and gagging didn't stop him. He gave me a mouthful and then some. Just thinking about that makes me so mad. Brice can treat me like shit when he wants to. I didn't speak to him for about a week after that.

Getting back to Christian, I tried to change the subject, but he wouldn't let me, and by now there was moisture between my legs and a craving that needed to be filled.

"Now, I know that would have you screaming out Brice's name if he did that shit to you. Oh, Brice . . . Oh, baby . . ." he said as he laughed hysterically. "I know that you can get loud. I remember that night in Georgia.

"Now it's my turn," he stated after he had calmed down.

"What do you mean?" I asked once I recovered from my embarrassment.

"Now it's my turn to ask the question. Let's see . . ." he said as he rubbed his hands together. "What is your sexual fantasy? Give me all the juicy details."

I sat there and seriously thought for a minute. "Okay. I got it. My sexual fantasy is to do it with two gorgeous, sexy men at the same time. I want to lay there and let them do whatever they want with me while my ankles and wrists are handcuffed to the bed."

Christian looked at me curiously for a moment with this lust-filled expression and, surprisingly, no comment.

Then I started laughing and said, "Gotcha."

"Mia, you had better stop this little game before I have to jump your bones in here," he said as he got up and went to the bathroom.

There was so much sexual tension going on that I let that alone for the remainder of the night, and Christian left shortly after that with a noticeable hard-on visible through his sweatpants. A large bulge at that.

But back to the present. Christian is here, and it is obvious that Vivica adores him. I'm glad that he grew up in a happy family after his mother died.

We didn't do too much the first day or so. Vivica fed us like we had never eaten before, we slept in and watched soap operas and *Jerry Springer*. I went out with Vivica to do some Christmas shopping, but I didn't have to shop for anyone because my presents were already wrapped and under the beautiful, live tree that we decorated. My first night there, Vivica and I went out and purchased this six-foot tree and spent the rest of the evening sipping hot cider, playing holiday music and decorating the tree with ornaments that had been in their family for years. When it was finished, we stood back and looked at our handiwork; it was beautiful. After that, Vivica entertained me with stories of Brice's and Christian's early Christmases.

Christian's second full day there, we went down to the church to help out with the day care center they ran. Vivica had told some of the church members that I was working towards my degree in education, so they asked me to come down and help out. I was more than happy to volunteer my services. The church ran a winter day care because they knew a lot of kids were at home during Christmas break with nothing to do while their parents worked. So they provided day care complete with activities, food and biblical studies. We had been lying around anyway, so we were happy to help out.

Christian and I arrived at Mission Rock Methodist Church dressed in jeans, T-shirts under flannel shirts, baseball caps and our lightweight jackets. It wasn't usually cold in Georgia, even at this time of the year. We decided to help with the preteens. I noticed the girls checking out Christian and giggling. It looked like he had some admirers; they had fallen in love with the handsome Marine. I glanced over at him, and he did look kinda cute. Those jeans were definitely fitting in all the right places, and his Timberland boots gave him a rugged look.

After introductions were made, the girls asked a lot of general questions about the military: "Do you have a gun?" "Have you ever killed anyone?" "What is it like?" "Have you ever fought in a war?" "Do you pick up a lot of girls?" Then we decided to play touch football. Outside we chose teams, and of course it ended up being the girls versus the guys. And guess who was the captain for the girls? Yours truly. We were going to kick some butt. We had hot chocolate waiting on the sidelines and a strong desire to win.

We were into the game and having a lot of fun. These kids were adorable. They hadn't gotten old enough to start acting grown yet. They were still at that awkward stage. Towards the end of the game, I found myself with football in hand running to the goal. Out of nowhere, Christian ran over and tackled me to the ground. All the leaves that lined the ground cushioned my fall. Christian fell right on top of me, and we were lying there laughing like little kids.

Christian wasn't making any great effort to get off of me or to take his right hand off my breast. I was telling him that he cheated and whatnot. Suddenly, I looked up into his eyes and he returned the stare intensely. It seemed like we looked at each other for a few minutes, though in reality it was only a few seconds. I could feel his heartbeat against my chest, and my own heartbeat was erratic. I could feel the warmth of his left hand on my thigh and the pressure of his right hand on my breast through my shirt. He looked at me and gently pulled the dry leaves out of my hair because my baseball cap had fallen off. For just a second his hand lingered on my cheek, and I thought that he was going to kiss me . . . For just a second. Then somebody called out my name, the spell was broken and Christian pulled me to my feet. I still couldn't forget what I had felt. For just a moment I felt and saw a longing, a yearning in his eyes . . . for me.

Shortly afterwards, the game ended with the boys winning by three points. For the remainder of the day, it seemed like Christian avoided me. When the last of the children rode off with their parents, we left as well. The drive over to Vivica's was mostly in silence with V-103 dishing out Christmas songs by the Temptations, James Brown and the O'Jays.

I tried to get Christian to lighten up by singing along with the radio, but he wouldn't budge. I told him that some lady at the church had asked about him. Actually, she thought he was Brice and was married to me. Once she realized we weren't married, she had tons of questions about the handsome, green-eyed Marine. Christian gave no response, so I didn't push it. By dinnertime he was back to his old self. I guess the fried catfish, corn on the cob, coleslaw and hush puppies that Vivica threw down perked him right up.

I have got to get a grip on myself. I've been having all sorts of crazy thoughts and ideas lately. All focusing on Mia, of all people—my best friend's wife. This is crazy, but Mia is driving me nuts with her smile, sexy body and genuine warmth. I knew it was a mistake coming here for the holidays, but Brice called and practically begged me to. When that didn't work, he gave me the guilt trip about how I would disappoint his parents. So I gave in. Don't get me wrong. I'm having a ball. This is one of the best Christmases that I can remember having in a long time. This is the most fun I've had in a while, and it's all because of Mia. But . . . I can't hide from the truth any longer. I've fallen in love with Mia.

You hear and read about this kinda shit all the time. In the movies, the guy who falls in love with his best friend's girl is always the bad guy. The villain. So I guess that's what it looks like I am. Hell, I didn't ask for this to happen. I don't even want to be in love. With love comes hurt and pain. I have never been in love with a woman . . . ever. I have never allowed myself to feel that emotion. Sure, I've cared about a few and even had some serious crushes when I was younger, but never love. Shit, I didn't ask for this.

These feelings that I'm experiencing are all new for me. I can't help it if Brice keeps throwing the two of us together. He knows what I'm like. I have desires and needs just like any other man. Mia is a beautiful, sexy lady, and just because she is his wife doesn't mean my system shuts down. I know I could have told him no, but to be honest, I enjoyed Mia's company as a friend in the beginning. Before I knew it, it had developed into much more for me. Yes, much more. And Mia is such a flirt. She knows that she is attractive, and I think sometimes she tries to test me, to test my loyalty to Brice. Mia is always doing something or saying something that turns me on and those big brown eyes . . .

Take the night she was asking questions about my sex life. I know I should have nipped it in the bud then, but I didn't. I wanted to have some fun with her and see her reaction. So I described in detail for her, graphic detail, something she wasn't getting from Brice. I knew my man—we had discussed it—and he didn't go there. By the time I finished, Mia was so embarrassed and so hot. It was funny actually. She wants to be so sophisticated sometimes, but she is still immature or she wouldn't do shit like that. I'm a man, and shit like that will make my nature rise.

Mia was so turned on that her nipples were poking through her thin T-shirt. That's another thing. She knows Brice doesn't allow her to go around without a bra, but whenever he's out of town and I come over, she doesn't wear one. I don't know what the girl is trying to do, or maybe she isn't trying to do anything. Maybe she just relishes her freedom to be herself when he's gone. Hell, I don't know. I just know that I am a full-blooded male and I have eyes. So if she puts it out there, I'm going to look.

I can't put the blame on anyone but myself. I realize I have to take responsibility for my actions too. Well, so far, I mean, there won't be any actions. Today, when we were playing touch football, I couldn't believe I almost kissed her. We were so close and she felt so good! I almost kissed her, and my hand lingered a little too long on her breast. But that won't happen again. That shit freaked me out! My best friend's wife! Man, that's fucked up! I decided today that I am going to have to control my feelings and distance myself from her gradually. I wouldn't do anything to hurt my man Brice.

Once we got back to the house I called Renee, the fox from church, and asked her out for tonight. I knew she'd been checking me out at church earlier today. I saw her looking at me out of the corner of her eye several times. I pretended not to notice her. And to be honest, I didn't, because my eyes were on Mia, but Renee has it going on. She has all the right equipment: big butt, big legs and big breasts. I think my chilling-out period is over. You have to be careful with these churchwomen. They want you to at least pretend that they are holier than thou, show them some respect, once it's said and done, they will drop the drawers and open wide just like any other woman.

Yeah, you can always tell when a sister wants you. For a second today, I thought I felt that in Mia. Anyway, Renee and I are going out tonight to the movies, and I bet she can make me forget all my problems.

I was right on target as usual. Renee was a little freak. By the time the evening ended, I had had her every which way but loose. She could have been an aerobics instructor, she was bending all kinds of ways. We were all over the bed, floor, her dresser, you name it. She definitely made my return from "chilling out" memorable. Yeah, she definitely knew how to work that ass. Renee had me screaming out like a little bitch. She could put a grind on you that made you want to slap your Moms. I fell asleep before my head hit the pillow, but when I woke up I made a big mistake. I made the mistake that all men fear.

Renee woke me up the next morning by kissing all over my face and chest. I guess she wanted some more before she left for work. But I was beat. She had worn me out. So I was still kinda half asleep when I pulled her close to me and called her Mia. The shit hit the fan. She called me every name but the name of God, and what could I say? I was busted. Cold busted.

This has been one of the best Christmases ever. Christmas has always been one of my favorite holidays, ever since I was a child
and Daddy would spoil me. I thought I would be miserable without
Brice by my side, but I'm not. I'm actually having a ball and enjoying my freedom. Hmmm. I talk to Brice every night. It's amazing
how I miss him when he's away. He always says the right things, and
I can feel his love pouring through the phone. But when he gets
home it can be a different story. I never know which Brice is coming home, my black knight or the mean muthafucka.

I have heard so many tales about the adventures of Brice and
Christian since I have been staying at my mother-in-law's. She is so
loving and warm, but that husband of hers can be a trip. He doesn't
say much, but when he does he expects everyone to jump at his beck
and call. He better get real. I take enough shit from his son. He has
been in poor health the last couple of years, but from what I heard
he was a mess. He is very proud of Brice and Christian, whom he
treats as his own. Women, he treats like servants.

Hopefully, Brice will be here in two more days. Christian has
been great as usual. Lately he has been seeing this lady from church.
It's very obvious that Renee likes him a lot. A few times, Renee and
I have gone out shopping for items for the church ball that is coming up in two days, just in time for me and Brice and Christian and
Renee to attend. I'm really excited about it because it's a fund-raiser
to help renovate the church. It will be a formal affair with a band
and ballroom dancing. Mama and I picked out this sexy black gown
and black shoes for me the other day when we were at Lenox Mall.

Mama is doing better, much better. She said that she still has her good days and bad days, but lately there have been more good days. She told me that she will never let her guard down because she will always be an alcoholic, but she realizes the answers to life's problems aren't found in the bottom of a liquor bottle.

I'm proud of her because she—hell, we—have seen some bad times since Daddy died. I thought I was going out of my mind a lot of days. I felt like I was the mama and she was the child. A stinking, pissy, vomiting drunk is not a pretty sight, especially when it is your own mother. I vividly recall coming home from school—I think I was in the eleventh grade at the time—to find Mama passed out on the sofa, reeking of liquor, vomit and her own urine. That day had actually started out good. I had been told that this cute guy, who had transferred from another school, liked me. Looking back, I was depressed and didn't know it then. Anyway, in the process of trying to clean up Mama, I got the vomit all over me. I finally sank to the floor and just cried. I thought I was losing it. My sanity, back then, came through reading and studying hard. I knew I had to get good grades in order to get a scholarship and escape her. I remember calling Uncle Larry and begging him, literally, to let me live with him and Aunt Ruth. I ate enough meals there that I might as well have moved my clothes in. Uncle Larry told me that Mama was having a rough time of things, but we were family, and family looked out for one another. So I stayed. I still never brought anyone home, out of embarrassment.

Yeah, I hated her, actually hated her at one point in my life. I knew when Uncle Larry found out I was marrying Brice, he thought I was trying to leave home to get away from Mama and her problems that became my problems as long as I lived there. I told him that wasn't true. I was marrying for love and a little lust. I didn't tell him the lust part though.

Speaking of parents, the strangest thing happened the other day when Mama and I went shopping. Parents, especially mothers, have a way of sensing when something is not quite right with their children. Mama is no different. I guess it was inevitable that she would suspect that there was trouble in paradise sooner or later. When we talked to each other every Sunday—I never missed a Sunday—I usually kept everything as upbeat as possible. Sometimes I would complain about feeling lonely when Brice traveled, or I would make light of some negative comment that Brice had made. Lately, he had gotten off the cooking comments and was focusing more on my weight. He was always telling me that when he touched me he wanted to feel some meat. He didn't want to make love to sticks and bones. Evidently, since he couldn't keep his hands off of me, my weight, or the lack of it, wasn't turning him off, that's for sure. He was still getting his and more. Brice is insatiable.

And it wasn't like Mama and I lived in the same state and saw each other all the time. So I was literally shocked as hell when she starting asking me these questions about Brice and Christian.

Mama and I had finally chosen the perfect black gown for me to wear to the church ball, and we were taking a much-needed break at Chick-fil-A before we started our search for just the right shoes. I was munching on my waffle fries, wondering if Brice would make it home in time for the party and thinking what a good day it had been for Mama and me. Mama had never been one for beating around the bush; she's very, very direct and straightforward. Still, her question caught me off guard.

"Mia, what's going on with you and Brice? Don't tell me nothing, because I know better."

I looked up from my fries and daydreaming and responded, "Mama, what are you talking about?"

"Girl, don't look at me like I'm crazy. Why isn't he here with you, and why are you always with Christian? Are you and him having an affair?"

I stared at Mama in utter disbelief. I didn't know whether to explode in anger or laugh or cry.

"Mama, you know Brice travels all the time. It's not like he has a nine-to-five job. He'll make it here. Don't worry. You also know the situation with Christian. The Matthews see him as a member of the family, a son. They sorta adopted him after his mother died. So Christian is home with his family, enjoying the holiday season, just like me. We just happen to be here at the same time, but not necessarily together. And, no, Christian and I aren't having an affair. My God, Mama, be for real. He's Brice's best friend. Christian and I are just friends."

"Ummm-humm, just friends. Right, tell me anything, you think I'm just an old lady who don't know any better."

"Mama, you and Daddy raised me right. And if I were having an affair, it wouldn't be with Brice's best friend."

"Yeah, and we also didn't raise a fool. That man cares about you, and it's more than as a friend."

I just looked down and murmured, "Whatever" because I was tired of explaining my relationship with Christian.

I looked up to find Mama staring at me.

"What?"

She hesitated for only a moment and said, "I don't know how to say this delicately, that's not my style, so I'll just say it. Has Brice been hitting you?"

My expression must have gone from shock, to dismay, to shame, to surprise and then to anger. "What are you talking about?"

"Mia, when you were trying on the dresses in the dressing room, I peeked through the curtain and I saw some fading bruises on your arms and legs."

I didn't know what to say or how to respond. For a moment, I was speechless and couldn't bear to even look at Mama. I could feel her piercing stare focused on me, anxiously waiting for an answer to her question.

When I looked back up and met her eyes for a brief second, just a second, I said, "Oh, those bruises. Mama you know how clumsy I can be at times. I fell down the stairs back at our apartment when I was taking out the trash last week."

She just looked at me ever so calmly and said, "Oh, I see."

There was an awkward silence as we each sat there lost in thought.

"Mia."

"Yes?"

"Remember, no matter how bad things may look, you can always come home. I'll always be here for you. You know that."

After lunch, I was able to pick out some shoes in record time. I wasn't being too picky; I wanted to get away from Mama and her accusations about Brice as soon as possible. I suddenly had a horrible headache. I tried to think back to the times the three of us, Brice, Mama and me, had been together. I tried to remember if she had seen or heard anything out of the ordinary. The one and only time she came to visit me in North Carolina, she had walked in from the Food Lion grocery store and seen Brice push me into our bedroom wall. Brice apologized to her profusely. He didn't to me.

He was upset because I had dropped off his lunch at his office, wearing shorts that he thought were too short. Mama and I had just returned from sightseeing, what little there is to sightsee in Fayetteville. We had stopped by the apartment and went back out to drop him off a sack lunch consisting of Mama's leftovers, since Brice complimented her so much the night before on her meal. When I walked in, I could feel the eyes taking in my body bit by bit as I greeted everyone and then walked the short distance to Brice's desk. I don't know what it is about military men; they all seem to be oversexed or something. You couldn't pay me to be a female in the armed services.

Anyway, when Brice arrived home that evening, Mama was at the grocery store down the block, picking up collards, neck bones and okra to make us dinner for the next day. She had a key to the apartment, so we didn't hear her when she came back with her packages. Brice had been screaming at me about my clothes and my flirting, let him tell it, and his temper got the best of him as usual, and he pushed me, no knocked me, into the wall. Mama walked in, in the middle of his tirade and him knocking me into the wall. I had only a slight bruise that time.

Of course, I pretended it was the first time something like that had ever happened, and I thought she believed me because it was never mentioned again.

You would think that Renee and Christian have known each other much longer than a week and a few days. They talked me into going out with them to Club Kaya's the other night and they were all over each other. I felt like a third wheel, and to be honest, I felt—I know it's crazy being that I'm a married woman—but I felt jealous. Christian was catering to her every whim. He wasn't ignoring me or anything, but I wasn't the center of his attention as I usually am. That night I also caught Renee watching Christian and me interact. I informed her the day that we went shopping that Christian is a good friend and nothing more. She looked at me like she still didn't believe me.

Anyway, that night we all got a little tipsy. Christian was being the gentleman and dancing with the two of us. He would take turns. It was my turn, and we had started out grooving to a fast song. We were really out of it, at least I was. When a slow song came on by Whitney Houston, the one that she remade and sang better than Dolly Parton ever did, I turned to go back to our table so that he could dance with Renee, since I saw her looking our way in anticipation, but Christian gently pulled me back onto the dance floor.

"Hey, can't I have this dance?" he asked as he put his arm around my waist and pulled me to him.

"Sure, I would love to dance with you," I said, doing a curtsy and almost falling flat on my face. Luckily, Christian caught me.

We were dancing and acting goofy. I don't know when the mood changed and we suddenly got serious. I had my arms around his back and my head on his chest, and he had his arms around my waist. We were listening to the beautiful sounds and lyrics of Whitney Houston and her angelic voice.

"Are you having a good time?" Christian whispered in a sexy voice.

I looked up and into his smiling, handsome face. "Yes. This past week has been so much fun. I feel so relaxed and peaceful."

"Good. I can tell that you're happy again."

I thought about that comment for a minute. "What do you mean that I'm happy again?"

Christian frowned before continuing. "I'm just saying that I know you and Brice have been going through some stuff lately. I'm glad that you're happy now, because you deserve it."

I stared deep into his eyes at those last comments and slowly laid my head back on his chest. We continued to dance in silence as my girl crooned out that song.

"Christian, why do you spend so much time with me? You don't have to, you know. I'm a big girl. I can take care of myself." I looked up into his face to await his answer.

Christian looked down at me and said something I will never forget.

"I think deep down you know the answer to that question already. Think about it," he whispered as the last notes of love and devotion were sang.

Once we made it back to our table, my face was flushed, and Renee looked from one of us to the other without saying a word. Christian excused himself to the restroom. Once he left, Renee kept looking at me with this . . . look . . . on her face.

"Renee, what's the problem?"

"Nothing, Mia. I'm trying hard to figure out how you haven't figured out that that man is in love with you. It shows in every thing he does. You must be blind or in denial."

"Renee, you are wrong. Christian is my husband's best friend in the world. There is no way. We are just good, good friends. That's all. Believe me, you don't have to feel threatened by me."

She didn't comment, but shrugged and turned away.

"Renee, I like you and would like for us to be friends. I personally think you are good for Christian. He needs a nice lady in his life."

"Girlfriend, he has a lady in his life, and you don't even know it."

Before I knew it, it was the evening of the ball. As I literally glided down the stairs in my black, sleeveless evening gown with black pumps and matching accessories, I felt like Cinderella going to the ball. My hair was styled in a classic French knot with a few curls framing my meticulously made-up face. Thanks to Fashion Fair, my makeup was applied flawlessly. I had gone to the mall earlier that day for a makeover and to have my nails done. Yeah, I knew I had it going on. I was "da bomb."

When I made it halfway down the stairs, Christian met me with a look of appreciation in his eyes that proved I was right. Yeah, I knew I was da bomb. You couldn't tell me anything. We posed for pictures as Vivica snapped away, taking yet another series of photos to go in her album. I swear this lady loved her memories.

Christian was looking too fine in his black tuxedo with black cummerbund. I knew Renee was going to freak when she laid eyes on him. The last few days they had been inseparable. I was happy for Christian because it appeared that Renee liked him, and she was sweet. Christian appeared to like her as well.

Renee and I had gotten closer after I reassured her that I loved Christian . . . just like a brother. I assured her that there wasn't any competition from me; I was the last person that she should worry about. I was happily married—most of the time. So now she was the closest thing that I had to a girlfriend.

I found myself somewhat jealous, which I thought was odd, because Christian hadn't had a lot of time for me the last few days. In fact, I had hardly seen him at all. If I didn't know better, I would have thought that he was avoiding me. Most of his nights were spent at Renee's. That explained why Renee was always smiling when I saw her. I had spent my last few days with Mama or shopping, which is my favorite pastime.

I had already come to the conclusion that Brice wasn't going to make it home in time for the ball, but I didn't care. I refused to let him put a damper on my fun this time. I knew I was going to feel like a third wheel, once again going to the party with Christian and Renee, but they insisted.

When we arrived in Midtown at the Marriott Marquis, which was hosting the evening's event, and went upstairs to the fifteenth floor, it was already in full swing, and the suite was breathtaking. Everyone on the decorating committee had outdone themselves with the mood and atmosphere they had created. The decorations were gorgeous and quite elegant with everything in black and gold. There were tables set up all over the room with the dance floor in the center. There was a definite atmosphere of intimacy and a festive mood in the air. The lights were kept low as a live band played oldies on the elevated stage. I knew or had met a lot of the people at the party and greetings and hugs were exchanged.

We finally found our table and were seated with a good view of the band. Like I thought, Renee couldn't keep her hands off Christian. They looked really cute together. Renee had on this sexy red dress. Christian seated himself between the two of us and was being the perfect gentleman, catering to our every whim. I had caught him staring at me a few times earlier and Renee's comments came back to haunt me.

"If I haven't told you already, you look beautiful tonight," Christian stated as he held my hand and we danced to a slow oldies song that I didn't recognize. I had tried to socialize and leave Christian and Renee alone for most of the night, but Christian wasn't having it.

"Why, thank you, sir. You look dashing yourself," I joked.

We danced silently with each other for a few more minutes. "Brice is a lucky man, Mia, and I love both of you like a brother and sister." He paused to look at me as if he was unsure he should go on.

"I think you are the best thing that ever happened to Brice, whether he knows it or not," he continued in a serious tone as he looked deep into my eyes.

"Thank you, Christian. I really appreciate that. That husband of mine can be a pain sometimes, but don't tell him I said that. I love him so much that it's scary. Yet sometimes I feel like I'm losing myself to him. You know Brice. Everything with him is just so intense."

Christian and I continued to dance, and I could feel the warmth of his hand on my back, the feel of his hand in mine and the pressure of his strong chest pressing against my breasts. I felt like I belonged there.

"Hey, can a man cut in and get a dance with his gorgeous wife?"

When I opened my eyes to match the face with the familiar voice, I looked right into my husband's handsome, sexy face.

I started smiling and couldn't stop and went into his eagerly waiting arms to finish off the dance. Christian stepped aside and disappeared back to our table to sit with Renee, who had returned from the restroom.

Brice looked and smelled so good. He was in his dress military uniform and he looked every bit the "man." I saw several female eyes and heads turned our way. He held me tight while he whispered how much he missed me and missed having me in his arms. I giggled and blushed like a schoolgirl because he still had that effect on me. We were totally oblivious to everyone else for the remainder of the evening. We danced, talked, held hands and sneaked kisses. Brice and I sat at the same table as Christian and Renee, but they might as well have been invisible. After introductions were made, we were totally into each other. My man was back and I couldn't wait to get home, in bed, and into his open arms.

You would have thought that he had been away forever. We came out from under our spell a few times to find Christian and Renee staring at us like we were two fools. We laughed and told them that we were happy to see each other. Brice even presented me with my Christmas present early, a beautiful sapphire and diamond tennis bracelet that I loved. Brice fastened it on my wrist, sealed it with a tender kiss and told me to always think of him whenever I wore it. It was such a sweet moment.

It was a wonderful, magical night; one that I will never forget. When we arrived home and were finally settled, I still didn't get any sleep that night. Brice and I were up all night making love; we couldn't get enough of each other.

Christmas came and went with the usual presents, excellent food, good cheer and laughter. At one point, I looked around and thought, *This is what Christmas is all about: sharing joy and love with your family.*

We were now back home and I had decided to take the quarter off from college because I wanted to focus on our marriage for a while. It was a hard decision to make because I can taste that degree. I'm so close, I can almost touch it, yet it seems so far. Brice doesn't give a damn if I graduate or not. He hasn't come right out and said that, but actions speak louder than words. He was glad to have me home again, fully dedicated to his needs. Therefore, everything for the most part was going well because I pretty much catered to Brice. I was always there, ready, willing and able in all aspects of our marriage. Even my culinary skills were improving.

I must admit that Brice was being more caring and trying to understand and appreciate my feelings. He was trying, and I gave him an "A" for effort. We were not seeing as much of Christian as we would have liked, at least I wasn't seeing him much. I guess Brice saw him on base, but he was keeping his distance from me. I guess he was busy with work and women. Hey, he had a life too.

So the months flew by, and the season changed from winter to spring. Vivica called one evening and invited us to a family reunion that they were having in Georgia, and she really, really wanted us to attend. We found ourselves back in Georgia for the weekend at her insistence.

It was predicted that it would be an unusually hot summer in Georgia that year. And I believed it because it was already hot and it was only the first of April. The day of the reunion had everyone running around trying to take care of last-minute details. The weather was beautiful and just right for a reunion in the park.

Brice had left without me to help out with setting up and I was going to ride over with my cousin Linda. I had invited Linda as my guest. Linda and I were around the same age and used to be really close, but over the years we had lost touch with each other. When I found out she was in town, we hooked up, doing the girl thing.

We caught up on our totally different lives. Linda was a flight attendant, flying all over the world, enjoying the single life. She informed me that she had run into one of my old boyfriends on a recent flight back to Atlanta. Greg was the graduate student who had whispered sweet words of love and devotion in my ear in between hot, passionate kisses that took my breath away. For a minute I had thought he was the one. Until he cheated on me. Cheated on me with a white girl. I walked in on him getting his groove on. Linda said Greg had asked about me. I informed her that I didn't have any time for the past. You can't change the past. She admitted that I looked happy in the married-woman role. I really wanted to talk openly to her about my marriage because I felt that I could trust her and I valued her opinion, but I just never got the chance. We were having so much fun. I realized I truly missed having a girlfriend to talk to and hang out with. Brice didn't like me hanging out.

We had gone shopping and picked out these cute, cool outfits to wear to the reunion. It was going to be a hot, muggy day, typical in Georgia, so we picked out these halter-style blouses with support bras on the inside, these cute shorts and tight stacked sandals.

Anyway, we arrived at the reunion and I finally found Brice nursing a cold beer and playing cards with some older men, much like the day I first met him. I went over to speak and I knew immediately that I was in deep shit. The expression that crossed over his face in just a few seconds was ice cold. I tried to excuse myself before he made a scene, but Brice grabbed my arm and told me to sit down and watch the card game. His eyes and his tight grip on my arm told me that there wasn't room for any argument. There wasn't anywhere to sit, so I ended up sitting in his lap.

Linda came over to get me a few times, but finally gave up when

Brice informed her that he wanted to spend some time with his wife. She frowned and walked off to talk with a group of women around our age. By now I was getting upset because he was treating me like a child who had to stay with her Daddy.

Finally, it was time to eat, and there was food galore. This family could throw down when it came time to cook and eat. We had stacked paper plates and were sitting at a table with one of Brice's cousins on his mother's side, and the man was literally gawking at me. If his eyes weren't on my chest, they were on my bare legs. And he was constantly licking his lips like he wanted to gobble me up. It was rude, but I didn't let it upset me. Brice, though, was mad as hell by now. He had barely spoken three sentences to me since I arrived, but he kept giving me one of those looks that told me he was not pleased. The entire day he kept an arm draped around my chair or an arm around my shoulder so that everyone knew I belonged to him, I guess.

Vivica rescued me when she came over to introduce me to somebody and took me away. I could feel Brice's eyes on me from across the yard, and he was not pleased. Linda had made her way back over to me also.

"Girl, what is wrong with that man of yours? He was shooting daggers my way."

"I don't know. He doesn't like what I'm wearing. He's kinda old-fashioned."

"Well, he had better get over it and chill. Girl, he should be proud that you have a body that looks like that. I mean, you don't look slutty or nothing. What's his problem?"

"I don't know, Linda. He's just very jealous. He doesn't like other men looking at me. Just drop it, okay?" I said, close to tears.

Linda looked at me and noticed my distress. "Mia, what's wrong? You know you can talk to me."

I wanted to tell her so badly, but when I opened my mouth to speak, words would not come out.

"My marriage—"

"Come on, Mia, let's go," Brice shouted as he roughly grabbed me by the arm and pushed me.

"Where are we going?" I asked as I looked apologetically at Linda standing there with her mouth agape.

"Just bring your ass to the car. I'm going to tell Moms that we'll see her at home," he said between clenched teeth.

I went obediently to the car, got in on the passenger side and was nervously waiting for him when he arrived a few minutes later. He got in and didn't even look in my direction nor say one single word the entire drive home. I sat as close to the passenger door as possible and tried to disappear.

As soon as we arrived home and stepped through the front door, all hell broke loose. My initial plan was to make myself as invisible as possible until he calmed down, but Brice wasn't having that.

He grabbed me by the arm, screaming, "What is this shit you're wearing!"

Before I could even answer his question, he was shouting and towering over me. "You know I don't allow you to wear shit like this. You see, that's why I didn't want you hanging with that slut Linda."

"Everybody is a slut, let you tell it. Brice, I can't talk to you when you are like this. Calm down . . . please," I screamed.

He shoved me backwards. "Don't tell me what to do. Do you hear me?"

By now I was crying hysterically.

"Brice, please don't. There is nothing wrong with this top."

"Oh, so there is nothing wrong with you showing off your body to every goddamn man you see? You know I don't allow you to wear shit like this. Take your goddamn ass upstairs and pull it off before I do!"

I stood there sobbing and staring at him in disbelief. *He doesn't allow . . . Who the hell does he think he is? . . . Certainly not my father.*

Brice was furious, red faced and ready to kick my ass.

"Mia, your tears don't affect me. Get . . . your . . . ass . . . upstairs! Do you hear me?"

I turned to run upstairs and murmured, "Yeah, I hear you loud and clear, muthafucka."

"What did you say? You don't disrespect me like that," he said as he grabbed me and slapped me twice, hard, real hard, with the back of his hand across my face.

I pulled away and was running, tripping, stumbling up the stairs, and he was right behind me. "Take off that goddamn shirt before I beat your fucking ass, Mia!"

I made it, somehow, upstairs to our bedroom and he started ripping my new shirt off and hitting me all over my shoulder and stomach as I tried to shield myself. I was defenseless. By now I was naked from the waist up, trying to cover up my exposed breasts, while he continued to rant and rave and beat me.

"You make me do this shit to you. You make me beat your ass. Goddammit, Mia. What do you expect when you act like a whore in my face?" Usually Brice hit me with an open hand. That day it was his fists that made contact.

By now I was curled up in a fetal position on the bed, sobbing uncontrollably, still trying to hide my breasts.

"Oh, no, you don't. Don't cover up now," he said as he grabbed my hands away from my breasts and roughly fondled them. I tried to pull away, and he grabbed my wrists and scratched my arms in the process. He knocked me back down on the bed and with his full weight on me, he forced my legs open as he used one hand to roughly yank my shorts and panties down to my ankles, tearing the shorts in the process.

"Brice, please stop. You don't know what you are doing. Stop, dammit."

By now he had his fingers roughly inside of me while he was still trying to fondle my breasts and take his penis out of his pants.

"Isn't this what you want, bitch?" he screamed in my face as he flipped me over on my stomach and started pushing his dick into my ass.

"I can't even stand to see your slutty face. You want to act like a slut, then I'll treat you like one."

"Stop, Brice. Leave me alone. You promised you wouldn't hurt me again. You promised," I screamed in a muffled voice because he had my face pressed against the bedspread as he continued to violate me. He raised his fists to hit me again when Vivica walked in.

"Oh my God! Brice, oh my God! Brice . . . what is going on? What are you doing to that child?" she screamed as she ran over to rescue me and cover me up with a green throw that was on the chair by the bed.

Brice turned to walk out of the room. "Mia had better learn to respect me, Mama. I'm tired of her mess. I'm tired of it. I wear the pants in my household."

I don't remember much of the rest of the evening. I vaguely remember Vivica helping to clean me up somewhat. I had bruises and scratches all over my body. My cheeks and eyes were swollen where he hit me. I'd probably have a black eye. I would have to sport the shades again. She put me to bed, and I must have slept for hours after my crying finally stopped, because when I awoke the open curtain at the window revealed it was dark outside and the upstairs was dead silent. I lifted my bruised and aching body out of the bed, a moan escaping my lips, and I painstakingly made my way to the bathroom and took a long hot shower and dressed in one of my long-sleeved shirts in order to hide some of the damage he had inflicted. I would be black-and-blue for days. This was the worst beating yet.

Vivica found me standing near the window when she came up to check on me. She had walked quietly into the bedroom with a serious scowl on her face. This was new. She typically presented a pleasant expression to everyone.

"Mia, come sit down, dear. We need to talk."

I slowly crossed the bedroom and sat down next to her on the bed, trying my best not to inflict any more pain to my already sore body.

"Mia," she said as she looked deep into my eyes, "how long has this been going on? I know this isn't the first time this has happened."

I looked down at the flowered bedspread because I couldn't bear for her to look at me in pity for something her son had done.

"Mia, talk to me. Over the last few months, I have grown to love you like a daughter, and this hurts me as much as it hurts you." Vivica looked away as though she were thinking of another time and place.

"Believe me, we didn't raise Brice to act like this. I can't believe he did this . . ."

There was a silence as we both sat on that tiny bed; two women who shared the stigma of spousal abuse. We were both lost in our own separate thoughts. Me, I couldn't believe this had happened again and I guess Vivica was thinking back to her younger days and the times it had happened to her with Brice's father. The apple doesn't fall far from the tree.

"Vivica, I appreciate your concern, but I really don't want to talk about it. I shouldn't have worn the outfit. I knew Brice didn't like me wearing stuff like that. Sometimes I can be so stupid. So stupid. I should have known better by now."

When Vivica spoke again, her tone and the anger reflected in her voice startled me for a minute. I had never heard her this upset. She was almost shouting. "Mia, don't let me ever hear you talking like that again. Do you hear me? You have the right to wear whatever you want, whenever you want. Brice is my only son, my only child and I love him dearly, but wrong is wrong. Marriage is supposed to be a uniting of two people, not ownership."

She got this hazed, distant, look in her eyes again and just started talking as if she needed to cleanse her soul. So I let her.

"I'm not trying to preach or judge you, Mia. Understand that. The good Lord knows what I have gone through with that husband of mine." At that, she looked at me as if she had forgotten what great secret she was supposed to keep.

"Baby, you have so much to offer this world and I don't want you to get caught up in thinking you somehow deserved to be beat, because you didn't. I don't know about Brice. I mean, we gave him everything when he was growing up. After all, he was our only child, and we doted on him. We knew there wouldn't be any siblings for him. So . . . we spoiled him. Maybe that was wrong, but you'll understand when you have children. You want them to have everything you were unable to have growing up."

Vivica sighed, wrung her hands, rose and walked over to the maple dresser that stood near the wall. "Brice was always demanding, possessive, and he's always had that temper. And I know my son has always loved women. I'm not blind to that fact, but as a mother we tend to overlook some things. Our children are always special in our eyes and can do no wrong.

"Yeah, I remember all those little girls who used to call here when he was in high school. Well, actually, it probably started when he was in middle school. These girls would call at all times of the night until we finally had to install his own phone line. I remember picking up the phone by accident one night and hearing this young girl crying her heart out over Brice. Apparently, she was no longer the flavor of the week, as the young kids say. She was begging, pleading with him not to break up with her. I can still hear the pain in her voice. I can still hear the things I heard my son say to that girl. A girl who had done nothing more than really like him.

"I recall coming home early one day from work because of a migraine headache. I used to suffer from them all the time. I found my son in his bedroom, sitting in a chair with his legs spread eagle, his drawers pulled down to his ankles, and this butt-naked girl, couldn't have been more than fifteen, squatting between his legs sucking his . . . well you know. His head was thrown back in ecstasy as he touched her between her legs. I silently closed the door and never mentioned it to him. I don't even know to this day if he saw me, because he never said anything to me about it. When they finished, they came downstairs as if nothing had happened upstairs. Brice kissed me on the cheek and said hello and the girl said, 'Hello, Mrs. Matthew,' and walked out the door.

"Over the years, girls came and went, and then when he grew into a man, women came and went. And I knew, I knew that my son didn't respect women. It was just a fact."

At that, Vivica turned and looked at me as if asking me to debate that fact. As if asking me to prove her wrong. I just looked back silently through tears.

"But then, Mia, when he met you, I thought that things had changed. I was so happy for him. I wanted him to experience real love at least once in his lifetime. He truly loves you, and I know that as a fact because I know my son. Mothers know. He doesn't let himself form too many attachments, but he loves you and Christian. Now, Christian is another story. They formed a bond during childhood that is yet to be broken. They are like blood brothers. No, Brice, Christian also for that matter, does not let too many people into his circle." She paused to catch her breath and continued on.

"Mia, I'm not trying to apologize for my son. I'm just trying to make you understand him or maybe make myself understand him and see how I failed him as a mother. His father was always so hard on him, constantly pushing him to be the best. Second place was never good enough, totally unacceptable. There are a lot of things that you don't know about my husband. He's a long way from perfect. We have to deal with what life throws our way. Good and bad. But I tried so hard with Brice."

With that I looked up and stated, "Vivica, you can't blame yourself for this happening. Brice is a grown man, responsible for his own actions. We all have choices. You either do what's right or what's wrong. You are so loving and sincere. You didn't fail Brice."

Vivica walked over and hugged me. When she saw that I was wincing, she released me.

"Baby, I can't tell you what to do. I love my son, and I want the best for him. I think, no, I know, that you are good for him, but . . . I don't know what to tell you."

"Vivica, I love Brice too, but he scares me so much sometimes. He has that fiery temper, and he is so possessive and jealous of my every action. When he gets really mad, he simply reacts, and that usually involves hitting me. I can't live like this. What am I going to do?" I cried as fresh tears ran down my bruised face.

Vivica just stared at me because she didn't have an answer any more than I did.

"Baby, why don't you come downstairs and get something to eat?"

"I'm not hungry."

"Mia, you should eat something. I've talked with Brice and he has calmed down. I don't know what got into him."

I was thinking, *Like father like son.*

Vivica finally convinced me to come downstairs and at least watch TV. I walked slowly and stiffly down the stairs with Vivica, and my heart was racing, about to jump out of my chest, because I was afraid that Brice would freak out again. I found Brice, his dad and two older men downstairs at the kitchen table, drinking and playing cards. Brice didn't even look up when I entered. Believe it or not, he was actually laughing and having a good time. It didn't matter to him that he had beat the shit out of his wife a few hours earlier.

I was thinking that I must have looked horrible with puffy, swollen eyes and a bruised face, a long-sleeved shirt on in the middle of the summer, but everyone pretended not to notice. I wanted them to notice and see what he had done to me.

"Mia, what do you want to eat, dear?"

"Nothing. I'm okay. I'll just get a Coke."

I walked over to the refrigerator to get a can of soda.

"Mia, get me another beer while you're over there."

I froze with my hand trembling on the refrigerator door because I wanted to scream at Brice to get it his damn self, but I knew better. I'm not a fool. I knew if I said something, anything smart to him, he wouldn't hesitate to jack me up in front of everyone.

Vivica softly said, "I'll get it, Brice."

"No, Moms, I want my wife to get it."

There was complete silence in the kitchen. You could have heard a pin drop. Brice still hadn't looked in my direction or even acknowledged me except for the beer comment. I knew that he was testing me and wanted to prove to his father and the other men that he had me under control.

I went ahead and opened the refrigerator, got a can of beer and walked over and slammed it on the table next to him without a word. I was tempted to shake it up and place it on the table, but I didn't have a death wish.

He continued to play cards without looking at me. "Put it in a beer mug, please, and don't slam it down again, Mia. Do you understand? I said, do you understand? Answer me."

"Yes, Brice, I understand perfectly," I said as I looked at the floor. I had finally gotten his attention, but was too afraid to even look at him.

I controlled my anger and tears and put the beer in a mug and placed it gently in front of him. Brice grabbed my hand and said, "Thank you, baby." For a few seconds, our eyes met. I saw victory and lust in his. In mine, I'm sure he saw defeat, fear and humiliation. I jerked away as if I had touched fire and walked into the living room and sat there watching, or should I say staring at, the TV for most of the night. After Brice's card buddies left, he came into the living room and glared at me. I didn't look up. He walked off with the comment that he wanted me in bed soon.

I sat downstairs for quite a while after everyone had gone off to bed, just thinking. Vivica had excused herself long ago, after once again apologizing profusely for her son. She hadn't beat me. Her damn son needed to be apologizing. He was the one who beat the shit out of me. He was the one who treated me like he owned me. Like I was his damn property. The house was quiet, dead quiet, and I could think. *Why me? What did I do wrong? Why can't he just love me?* Finally, I walked slowly up the stairs to our room; I couldn't put it off any longer. If I didn't go, Brice would only come down and get me. So why put it off? I knew what he wanted. Whenever he hit me, afterwards he always wanted sex. It was like the violence turned him on.

When I got upstairs, the lights were off and Brice was in bed, lying on his back with a thin sheet between me and his nakedness. I changed into a T-shirt with a lot of effort, and I climbed between the sheets as far away from Brice as possible. I had no sooner lain down when Brice slid over next to me with his chest pressed up against my back. My entire body instantly froze. I felt his hands, the ones that had hit me, as they started to search for the gap between my skin and the T-shirt. He whispered in my ear, "You won't need your shirt or panties tonight. Get up and pull them off."

He got up to lock the door, and he turned and looked at me. "Now, Mia." I got up, trembling, obediently pulled off my shirt and panties, with little or no emotion, and laid back down with my legs spread eagle. He opened my stiff legs even farther and for most of the night was all hands, tongue and mouth all over my bruised, aching body. He had the bedsprings squeaking, my legs spread as he was humping and grinding inside of me. My mind was screaming, no, no, no, over and over again. I lay there with my eyes closed, tuned everything out, and took it as he moaned and groaned in my ear.

The following afternoon we left for home. I don't know why I even got into the car with him. I thought briefly about going home to Mama across town, but I was scared. I knew he wouldn't let me stay in Georgia without some major drama. I belonged to him, or so he thought. He had won. He had broken me. I didn't give a fuck anymore, and I was scared as hell of him. I didn't want to get beat down again. The drive back was mostly done in silence. Long silent miles. I answered his questions with as little communication as possible when I wasn't pretending to be asleep. I couldn't stand the sight of him, his smell or his touch. Brice made my skin crawl.

Mama always said that God didn't give us more than we could handle. Well, I had come to the end of my rope. I couldn't handle any more. All I had done wrong was love this man with all my heart and soul. And . . . this was the thanks I got.

24   Christian

Quit putting me in the middle of all your drama! Why is it that two people who love each other can't seem to get along? Damn. Somebody answer that for me, please. Don't put me in the middle of all your shit.

That's why I decided to keep my distance, at least that's one of my reasons. I'm not married to them or their many problems. And I'm not a fucking marriage counselor either. At first, my distancing myself was working, but then Mia would come and see me at my apartment. What was I supposed to do? Turn her away? I think not. I could never turn my back on Mia.

Here's the scenario. I came home one day, about two weeks ago, after a hard day of work, and the only thing I could think of was a long, hot shower, but I saw this lovely angel sitting on my stoop waiting for me. So what did I do? I let her in; I let her vent and listened as her friend. That was the least I could do.

I don't know what happened to them after Christmas. I thought Christmas had put them back on the right track, but some kind of serious drama happened when they went back for the second visit. My man will tell me about it when he is ready, but it doesn't take a rocket scientist to figure out what happened. He tapped that ass again.

Anyway, Mia will show up wanting to talk now and then. The last time this happened, I came home to find her sitting on my stoop crying silently. No words were spoken. She looked up and saw me, and I helped her up and opened the door to my apartment. When we got into the apartment she completely fell apart. She was crying about how Brice wanted her to have his baby and how she didn't want to and how she was still taking her birth control pills and he didn't know that and if he ever found out . . . well, she didn't want to think about what would happen if he ever found out. Mia went on and on about him, sobbing and asking why he hated her so. I was thinking, *There's a thin line between love and hate.*

I assured her that he didn't hate her because Brice was crying on my other shoulder about how much he loved this girl but how he always let his temper get the best of him. Brice didn't want to lose her. That was his greatest fear. He thought having a baby would bring them closer together and make them a real family. He went on and on about how Mia was so immature and needed to grow up and be a real woman for him. He said that he didn't need a little girl. I wanted to tell him that he had known her age, known all of this, when he married her. I kept my comments to myself, though I had plenty to offer in the way of my observations. Like, first of all, beating the hell out of somebody wasn't going to bring the two of you closer together, or if Mia would quit her flirting and making the man crazy to begin with, there wouldn't be so much conflict.

But, hey, I listened and was a sounding board for Mia and for Brice. The last time Mia came over she was upset about the baby issue, but she left laughing and almost back to normal. I told her, I don't know why I did, that I would talk to Brice for her. That pleased her.

25 Brice

I know now what it means and feels like to walk on eggshells because that is exactly what I have been doing around Mia since we returned from Georgia. I have apologized over and over and over, but I can tell that Mia is still afraid of me. I think the fear has overpowered the love that she felt for me. I think that the only emotion she has now is fear. I don't want my wife afraid of me, regardless of the advice Daddy gave me years ago. When Mia looks at me I want to see love, affection, admiration, lust and respect reflected in her eyes, anything but fear in her pretty brown eyes.

Mia asked me if I would go with her to see a marriage counselor. I wanted to tell her what I was truly feeling, which was absolutely, positively "hell no," but instead I told her I had to think about it. We don't need anyone to fix our marriage for us. We can do that for ourselves. I don't want to tell some shrink intimate details about myself so that he can blame everything on my parents. I'm not crazy. I just need to control my temper.

Moms called the other night. It's been two months since we were in Georgia. She ended our conversation advising me to look deep within myself before it's too late. She said I needed to confront Daddy and get some answers from the source.

Today started out as one of those days that goes on and on and on . . . just like that annoying Energizer bunny. I couldn't focus or concentrate in any of my classes. Even my favorite professor, Dr. Hembrick, couldn't break through my thoughts today as he discussed the needs of the exceptional children in the ever-changing educational system. So, thankfully, I had only one more class to make it through. And then . . . I could put all my stress and headaches behind me for the entire weekend. Heaven.

My wonderful, sexy husband was taking me away for a stress-free, romantic, relaxing weekend. Brice surprised me the other day when he suggested that we get in the car and keep driving until we ended up somewhere, anywhere.

He wanted to get away from Fort Bragg as much as I did. So I could hardly wait to hit the road, but unfortunately I couldn't concentrate on anything else.

Whenever we went away, it was always a wonderful, magical time for us. Brice devoted all his time and energies into pleasing me both mentally and physically. It was like I had the Brice that I had fallen head over heals in love with and we were totally into each other. It is almost like a honeymoon.

As I alternated between checking the huge white clock over the classroom door several times and trying to listen to Dr. Hembrick, I could hardly remain still in my seat. Finally, class was dismissed. Damn, one more class to go until freedom and Brice.

I still had several more minutes before my next class, which just happened to be in the same building, so I casually strolled over to talk to a few classmates that I knew from other classes. Their conversation was always the same. These women talked about who was sleeping with whom, what they were going to buy at the mall for the fraternity party over the weekend or if some basketball player, football player, whoever, was going to call them back after screwing them the previous weekend. I couldn't relate, and therefore, I always felt like an outsider even though I was around their age.

Their conversations seemed like they had happened to me light-years ago. Hell, I was a married woman with a very demanding, passionate husband. My biggest concerns were to not make him upset with me and to obtain my degree so that I could gain some sort of independence. I desperately needed financial independence. My husband refused to let me work in any form or fashion. Therefore, I received an allowance from him each week, like a child. If I ran out of money, too bad. And he wouldn't bend in his decision. He said I needed to learn some discipline. So I never quite figured out if I envied them for their carefree lifestyles or pitied them for their lack of knowledge about real life and responsibilities.

Anyway, when I looked up the narrow hallway, I saw Brice walking towards me. That came as a shock, and I did a double take, because it was kind of an unspoken rule that the campus was my territory, my domain. The campus of State University, strategically placed about three miles from base, was one place I felt I could be myself and not have to worry about my every action. Actually, it was my sanctuary.

I don't think Brice had ever visited me on campus. He used to tell me all the time that he was going to buy me a pager so that he could get in touch with me while I was on campus. I lied and told him that it was policy that pagers had to be turned off on campus. Hell, he wasn't going to monitor my every move. It wasn't like I had anything to hide anyway. Guys didn't try to talk to me on campus because they all knew who my husband was, and if they didn't know then they soon found out. So I was usually kept at a hands-off distance. There were a few men who were nonmilitary who I chatted with casually. Yet Brice was so afraid that I was talking to some college boy that he was forever questioning me over nothing. I barely had any friends. Hell, I didn't have any.

Brice was walking my way, dressed in Marine fatigues, motioning for me. I quickly walked over to meet him, and I could feel the eyes and stares checking out my man from head to toe. He did look finnnne! I still loved to see him in uniform. It was so sexy. My man had the body and the looks. Yeah, Brice had it going on. When I wasn't angry with him, he could still make me weak from just looking at me that certain way. I always knew what was in store for me later that night. Good loving.

"Hi, what's up?" I asked as he led me, by the elbow, over to a corner that housed pay phones. It was somewhat private.

"You couldn't wait to begin our weekend, huh?" I asked as I flicked a piece of lint off of his shirt. Since our return from Georgia, he had apologized and treated me like a queen for weeks now.

"Listen, baby, that's what I'm here about," he stated as he playfully penned me against the wall.

"What, are we leaving later than planned?"

"No, I have to go out of town this weekend. Sergeant Brown's wife was in a car accident and he can't make it and I . . ."

"And you just kinda, sorta volunteered your services," I said as my eyes began to water and tears threatened to spill forth.

"Dammit, I knew you'd have this reaction. Listen, Mia, I have a J-O-B and responsibilities! That's reality, not this college shit. I don't have the luxury of sitting on my ass all day attending classes. You'll find that out once you get a real job."

As I tried to control my tears, I said, "You still don't get it, do you, Brice? I try so hard to please you. I really do. I want to be the wife that you want me to be, and I don't ask for much in return."

I took a deep breath to continue on. "All you do is take, take, take. You are so full of yourself. What about my needs? I wanted to go away this weekend. I really wanted, no I really needed, to spend this time with you."

"Mia, what do you want me to do? Hell, I explained the situation. What more do you want from me? Get Christian to go with you to a movie or something."

"I can't."

"You can't. Why not?"

"Because."

"Because what, Mia?"

"He's not you, Brice. Don't you understand you're my husband, not Christian? Christian does have a life."

As Brice stood before me, he threw his hands up in the air in exasperation. "I give up, baby. I repeat—listen good now—I am going out of town this weekend on business. Accept it and deal with it," he said in a tone that indicated he was through and disgusted with the entire situation.

"Fine. Whatever," I angrily said as I attempted to pull away from him and walk away.

"Mia, you see, I can't talk to you when you are like this. Why all the drama?" he angrily asked as he grabbed my left wrist before I could walk away.

"Let go of me," I said as I struggled to loosen his tight grip on me and keep my voice down.

"Mia, cut all the drama before I . . ."

"Before you what, Brice? Kick my ass? Go on, hit me. That's not your style to do that in front of a crowd of people."

He just stared at me.

"You like to hit me behind closed doors, remember?"

Brice continued to stare at me for a few minutes with this strange expression, and I actually thought he was going to knock me down.

"I'm really sorry that you feel that way about me. We have had more good times than bad. I was going to say, before you revealed your true feelings about me, that I will make it up to you."

"Don't do me any favors. Okay?"

For a second, just a second, I saw this angry look cross his face, and then I guess he realized where he was. Brice released me with a slight push.

"Fine, whatever, Mia. I'm out of here. You get your act together before I come home on Sunday or I will deal with it. That's a promise."

He turned just like that, with me silently crying as I leaned against the wall, and he strutted away.

"I'll call you . . ."

"Brice," I yelled as I ran from around the corner.

He just held up his hand, kept walking and never turned around to even acknowledge my presence. Brice had dismissed me.

"I said I'll call you, Mia."

I slowly walked back to the corner and cried fresh, silent tears. He'd call me.

When I finally composed myself, I gathered up my book bag from the floor and headed home. I had already missed twenty minutes of my last class. What was the purpose of going to it now? As I turned the corner, I ran straight into this very attractive, sexy soldier. He gently grabbed my shoulder to keep me from falling. I had seen him around. I think his name was Malcolm. I had also heard of his reputation. He was a ladies' man, probably with nothing going for him except his looks and gorgeous body.

"Are you all right? I couldn't help but hear some of your conversation."

"Thanks, I'm fine," I said through tears.

"You're Mia, right? I've seen you around."

I nodded my head as I stared at the handsome soldier and fellow student.

"Listen, would you like to get some coffee and talk or something? I know that you don't know me, but you seem pretty upset. You look like you need a friend."

"No, no thanks," I said as I quickly walked away with his eyes boring into my back.

As I walked away from the pay phones for the second time that day, my thoughts drifted back to the previous day's argument with Mia. I had tried calling last night and first thing this morning, and the phone just rang and rang and rang. If I knew Mia, she was there, simply not answering the phone because she knew it was me. I thought about having Christian check up on her, but I was so sure that she was there that I didn't even bother. Mia knew the deal by now. I didn't care how angry she might be at me, she still knew that I didn't play. She knew that I would tap that ass in a second.

As I walked back to our display area that consisted of brochures and pamphlets advertising the advantages of enlisting in the Marines, I observed my fellow coworkers. I had worked with Sergeant Barnes before. He was fortyish, with a good sense of humor and was a career soldier. Sergeant Taylor, on the other hand, was new, and I hadn't figured him out yet. Taylor was close to my age and had checked out practically every female college student that passed within a mile radius of our table. Yet he had a wife and two children back on base. I wasn't trying to be judgmental because I had been there and done that for many years myself, but there was one difference at the time—I'd been single.

As I approached the table, I saw this young lady that he had been flirting with slip him what I assumed was her phone number and dorm room number before she slithered off. This was the same little freak that had tried to kick it with me when he was in the restroom. I had flashed her the wedding band and she had gotten the picture loud and clear.

Taylor just smiled at me like, *Yeah man, I'm getting some of that later tonight.* He didn't have to tell me. I knew the drill. I had had enough of these young women on numerous occasions on college campuses all over the country, including State University. A quickie between their first and third class or before lunch. They were all the same. They wanted to get off fucking a Marine. I simply gave them what they wanted. It was a thrill for them, and believe me, I didn't suffer any. The things some of these girls would do. I remember these two roommates who liked threesomes . . . I came out of my haze with a smile on my face and walked over to our table.

Barnes was the first to speak. "Did you get your wife on the phone?"

"No, man. I don't know where she is. We had a pretty heated argument before I left, so she's probably not answering on purpose."

"Women, can't live with them, can't live without them," we all chanted in unison.

Taylor just smirked as he said, "Well, gentlemen, I won't be joining you for dinner tonight. I have another engagement."

Barnes asked, "Oh, that's what they call it nowadays? An engagement? Man, you can be straight with us. You are going to get you some young stuff. I saw that girl slip you her number, and with that tight sweater she had on, with her titties about to bust out and that short-ass skirt, I don't think you will be doing anything but having some good old-fashioned, hot, sweaty sex."

We all laughed at that.

"So, Brice, I hear you are still pretty much a newlywed," Taylor stated.

"Yeah, I guess you could say that. I've been married almost three years."

"And you should see his wife. You talking about a looker. Mia is an angel. She's a beautiful lady inside and out."

Taylor continued. "Yeah, I remember those days before our two children put an extra twenty pounds on my wife, Anita."

Barnes said, "I was just telling Taylor that I could tell him some tales about you in your single days that could put some hair on his chest."

Barnes continued as he laughed and shook his head. "This man was a serious player. Him and Christian—you've met him—could show you some things."

I said, "But now I'm married and I've settled down."

"Man, I'm proud of you. When I first heard that you had tied the knot, me and the fellows bet that you wouldn't last a year before you were screwing somebody's daughter."

"You hold on to Mia. She is truly a good woman if she can change a zebra's stripes."

Taylor laughed and said, "Well, I give you mad props, man, but personally, what my wife doesn't know isn't going to hurt her. Men were not born to be monogamous. Tonight, I'm getting my groove on. Can I get an amen to that?"

We all laughed and shook our heads at this fool as a few students curiously strolled up to our table to ask questions. Before the day was over, we had a few serious prospects. The Marines were always looking for a few good men and women.

Mia is a full-time student this quarter, so she is at the university most of the day in classes or studying at the library, and I am still traveling with the Marines. So, actually, we don't see a lot of each other. I have a feeling that's fine with Mia. She doesn't complain like she used to about me being away all the time. When I'm at home, we are so polite to each other. Marriage is hard work. I never imagined it would be this hard, though. My child bride is definitely a handful.

I feel like I am losing her sometimes, and that scares me because I love her so much. I can't imagine life without her now. Mia is as much a part of me as my right arm. I know I have a funny way of showing my love, but I do love her dearly. Christian has got to be sick of me crying on his shoulder, but I have to vent my feelings to someone before Mia drives me crazy.

Christian has given me some great insight into my marital problems. That's cool, because he is friends with Mia too, and he is impartial and unbiased. He's on the outside looking in. He's not right up here in the midst of all this craziness. I try to follow his advice and stop myself when I'm being too overbearing or jealous. Those are my main problems with Mia. Actually, things were improving somewhat around my household. We had reached a stalemate, until the other night.

It was a Friday night, and Mia and I were both at home for a change. I suggested that we meet Christian at this local Marine hangout in town for a few drinks to unwind and start off the weekend right. Christian had called earlier and said he would be there around nine o'clock. Normally I would have gone by myself and left Mia at home. See, I was trying. I knew she would be lonely sitting at home alone on a Friday night.

I could tell Mia was glad to be getting out of the apartment. Once she had changed into jeans and a State University T-shirt, we were on our way. Christian was already seated at our usual table, and I noticed it had already started to get crowded with the usual military types, privates out for a fun night on the town. Officers didn't usually hang out there, but Christian and I liked the atmosphere. I noticed when we first walked in that there was a table of privates, two females and a male, who were around Mia's age, sitting at a table over near the corner, drinking beer. One of the women waved at Mia, and Mia smiled and waved back shyly. Mia said that the girl was in one of her classes at the university.

Once we joined Christian, Christian and I were soon lost in military talk and sports. Mia was quietly sitting there by my side with her head resting on the table, bored silly. I noticed that she kept looking over at the table where her classmate was sitting and having a good time from the sounds of the laughter that was coming from their direction. Christian noticed this too.

"I guess our conversation isn't stimulating enough for Miss Mia tonight," Christian joked. Mia smiled in his direction without answering. I noticed how relaxed they had become with each other.

Mia excused herself to go to the bathroom, and on her return back to our table, she stopped by her friend's table to say hello. They were all laughing, Mia included, about something. Mia didn't stay long and was soon back at my side. Later, her friend came over and asked if Mia wanted to sit with them for a while. Mia was getting ready to say no when I surprised her by encouraging her to go. See, I was trying.

She walked over, and Christian and I talked some more and drank more beer, and I would glance over in Mia's direction every now and then. She was having fun. I hadn't seen her smile and be happy like that in a long time. They had put some money in the jukebox and were playfully dancing now. Mia was doing her thing as well. I sat back, gulped down the rest of my beer and watched Mia slide across the small dance floor.

Christian and I were winding down because he had plans for later that night, which I'm sure included a woman. He didn't tell me about his escapades like he used to. Also, I didn't think there were as many anymore. I walked the short distance over to the dance floor to tell my wife good-bye and tell her she could hang out with her friends for a while longer if she wanted to. I was worn out and was going home to bed and some much-needed sleep.

Mia was still on the dance floor, giggling as they danced around with the only male in the bunch. I had seen him, actually all of them, around on base. I think his name was Malcolm. He was a tall, dark-skinned brother who already had a reputation on base as being a maverick. He had the usual arrogance that some of these hotshots projected. There wasn't a lot of interaction going on between him and Mia because she was mostly talking to her girlfriend. I noticed Mia had a beer in her right hand; Mia usually never drank anything because she had seen the effects of alcohol firsthand on her mother, but tonight she was unwinding. That was cool.

"Hey, come here, baby," I said as I gently pulled her into my arms away from the dance floor and noise.

"Listen, I'm beat, so I'm going home to bed, but you can hang out for a while if you want to."

Mia looked at me with an expression of total, complete surprise because she thought I had come over to tell her it was time to leave.

She said, "Okay, if you are sure?" as she looked into my eyes and leaned her body seductively into mine.

I still had my arm around her waist. "I'm sure if you will give me a slow dance before I leave."

Mia gave me this shy smile as I held her in my arms and we danced to the music. She felt and smelled so good. Fresh and innocent. And it felt so right with her in my arms. To be honest, I wanted to take her home with me and make sweet love to her. She had turned me on, and sex had been missing in our relationship lately, but a few minutes later Christian and I were out of there.

As soon as I hit the door, I was taking off clothes, leaving a trail down the hallway, and I went straight to bed and was out as soon as my head hit the pillow. For some reason, I don't know what made me, but I woke up from my deep sleep around one a.m. according to the digital clock. I reached out for Mia and she wasn't there. From the looks of her side of the bed, she hadn't been there, either. I looked sleepily at the clock again and decided to call the bar, which didn't usually close until around three a.m. on the weekend. I was worried and wanted to know what was up. I called the bar. The manager-owner, Curtis, was a friend of mine. He told me that I had just missed Mia. She had just walked out the door with Malcolm, and she was pretty buzzed. The other ladies had left at least two hours earlier. I lay back down and waited.

28 Mia

When Malcolm dropped me off at the apartment I knew that Brice was going to be pissed, but I was hoping that he was sound asleep and I could slip into bed unnoticed. When my other two friends decided to leave, I wasn't ready to leave yet because I was having too much fun. I hadn't danced, laughed and had so much fun in a long, long time. I felt like a twentysomething person again. I felt young and not tied down with a mountain of problems. And the beer was also adding to my ecstasy since I wasn't use to drinking. I knew I had a slight buzz, but I didn't care. So when they left, Malcolm agreed to stay behind and make sure I got home safely. He wasn't ready to leave either. Hell, Brice wanted me to enjoy myself, and it wasn't really late yet. I was going to stay only another hour.

Malcolm and I talked and danced and the time just flew by. He was so easy to talk to and had all kinds of crazy tales about growing up in New Orleans. He said that even as a young boy he always wanted to be a Marine. He saw it as exciting and dangerous. I knew I was flirting a little too much, and his hands were "accidentally" landing and touching places where they shouldn't when we were dancing, but I didn't care. I was free. I didn't have a care in the world.

Malcolm was very attractive and sexy. The brotha was a solid six-foot, with dark chocolate skin, bald head and these sensuous lips. He had it going on. Sex was nonexistent in my household lately mainly because I wouldn't give Brice any. Sex was the one thing I could control unless he simply forced himself on me. So it had been a while and I was getting turned on. My nipples were hard as rocks. It had been a long time since a man other than my husband had

made me feel attractive and sexy. I could tell by the sultry look in
Malcolm's eyes that he was definitely turned on. When the dancing
and horsing around got a little out of hand, I decided he had better
take me home. At one point, he had pulled me onto his lap and his
hands were inching a little too far up my back and near my breasts.
I could feel his hard-on through his black jeans, so I knew it was definitely time to go.

In the car, on the drive over to my apartment, Malcolm was talking nonstop. He was totally out of it. "Listen, Mia, I really like you.
I mean . . . I know that you are married and all, but you know we
hear rumors on base. Sergeant Matthews can be a cold-blooded
muthafucka. He has a reputation on base—you don't mess with him.
When he was a drill sergeant, he made life a living hell for a lot of
privates coming up through basic training. But you've got to give
him his props. He's the man. He's well respected on base. I guess we
have a love-hate relationship for him."

"Why are you telling me all this?"

"Mia, like I said before, I like you. You can't be happy with him.
He's too controlling. We are two adults, and from the vibes I've been
getting tonight, you like me too. I could make you happy and make
you feel good. No one would have to know. No strings attached. I
wouldn't want to get you in trouble with your old man."

He was able to pick up on how unhappy and in need of love I
was, so I couldn't even be mad. I politely told him no thank you, got
out of the car and ran upstairs to our apartment. As my no luck
would have it, Brice was not asleep and was waiting for me. He
didn't waste any time.

"Mia, where the hell have you been? It's almost one thirty."

I didn't say anything for a few seconds. "Brice, I was at the bar
where you left me."

"What could you have possibly been doing there after one in
the morning?" he asked as he took a deep breath and tried to remain calm.

My next sentence was my big mistake. "I was hanging out with the girls and talking," I said without looking at him, getting ready to go into the bathroom.

The next thing I knew, Brice jumped off the bed, grabbed me by the shirt and shoved me into the dresser.

"Don't you even try to come up in here with those goddamn lies. I know that you left the bar with Malcolm."

"What were you doing? Spying on me?"

"No, what were you doing, Mia? Do you want him to fuck you? Isn't one soldier enough for you?" he asked as he approached me again. "I am so sick of your shit, girl."

I don't know what came over me. All I knew was that I couldn't and wouldn't let him hit me again. I couldn't take it anymore. My instincts took over. I ran out the front door and down the steps, sobbing hysterically. I didn't know where I was going, but I just kept running as if my life depended on it. I knew I couldn't stop. I vaguely remember Brice running after me, but he wasn't dressed, so he stopped at the stairway screaming for me to come back. I was murmuring, over and over, something about how I wasn't going to let him hit me again.

I ended up frantically pounding and crying at Christian's door. His neighbors must have thought a madwoman was in the building. I was crying and couldn't catch my breath. Snot was running down my face, my sleeve was torn, but I kept banging on the door for Christian. I didn't care what woman he had up in there. And I didn't care what they were doing. I just had to get in, see him and feel safe and secure.

Christian finally opened the door with hasily pulled on pajamas, no shirt, looking sleepy and perplexed. I flew inside and into his arms. I had my arms around his neck, my head on his stomach, sobbing uncontrollably.

"Christian, I can't take it anymore. He did it again. I can't take it."

"Wait a minute. Slow down," he said as he led me over to his sofa. By now I had completely collapsed in his arms.

"Now, Mia, calm down. Tell me what happened," he said as if he were talking to a baby while he smoothed my hair out of my face.

I took deep breaths to control myself and said, "It's Brice again. He is so jealous, and he thinks that I have something going on with Malcolm, and he was mad and started pushing and shoving and was going to hit me, and I had to get away."

Finally I was totally out of breath. "You were the only person that I could think of to come to."

Christian sat back on the sofa with his hands on his head. "Damn, what the fuck is wrong with my man?"

By now I was sobbing softly and lying against his chest while he rubbed my back. "Christian, can I stay here tonight? I'm not going back over there. I don't know what he might do."

Christian looked at me like I had asked him to murder someone for me. He hesitated and said, "Okay, Mia. But first I have to call Brice and let him know that you are here. Okay?"

I didn't say anything, so I guess he took that as a yes. He released me and walked over to the phone. He turned his back to me, and I really didn't hear most of the conversation. The phone call was short and sweet and he hung up.

With a frown, he walked back over to the sofa where I was still lying. He looked as bad as I felt. "Christian, if you want me to go, I will."

"Mia, I want you here. Really I do. It's just that . . ."

"I know this puts you in an awkward position, what with you and Brice being best friends."

"Mia, I'm your friend too."

I sat there and thought about that for a few minutes. "You know, you always say that, but I know and you know that your loyalties and ties lie with Brice. I know that and knew that from the very beginning. But there is going to come a day when you are going to have to make a choice. Then what, Christian? What will your choice be?"

With that I got up and excused myself to his bathroom. When I got out, Christian had one of his long button-down shirts laid out for me to sleep in and a blanket and pillow on the sofa for himself.

"Thanks again, Christian," I said as I came back from changing into his shirt. It smelled of Christian. Fresh, clean and masculine.

"You know I can't put you out of your own bed. I'll take the sofa. Please."

"Are you okay now? Is there anything I can get for you?" Christian asked with deep concern etched into the frown lines on his face.

"No, I'm fine. I'm okay. Go to bed. You look tired and I'm sorry about all that stuff I said earlier. I was just talking crazy. You have been a good friend to me from day one."

"Listen, Mia, if you want to talk, you know I'm here for you."

I shook my head because I was afraid if I said anything else the tears would flow again and never stop. Christian took that as his signal to exit. After he was gone, I laid on the sofa, tossed and turned, unable to sleep. I tossed and turned back and forth. Finally, after about an hour of that, I got up and walked into Christian's bedroom and pulled back the sheet, getting into bed next to him.

"Mia, what the hell?"

"Can I sleep in here? Please."

"I don't know. This isn't right."

"I need you right now. I just want to lie here next to you, that's all. Nothing more."

"Mia, Brice wouldn't . . ."

"Fuck Brice. Think about me for a change and how I feel."

"Okay, okay," he said reluctantly as he covered me up with the sheet.

I snuggled under the sheet and slid my body over near Christian with my back to him, and there was complete silence for a few minutes.

"Christian?" I asked. "Could you hold me?"

He didn't say anything. He simply put his arms around my waist and pulled me close into a spooning position, with his stomach pressed against my back. My shirt had come up around my waist, and my legs and panties were up against him and I could feel his warmth and his hardness, but nothing sexual happened. I remember saying good night and falling asleep safe and sound in his arms.

ia stayed with me for the remainder of the week before Brice convinced, begged her to go home. I don't know what promises he made this time, but she went. He had called constantly the first few days, but Mia wouldn't have anything to do with him, and my apartment looked like a floral shop.

The first few days, we both pretty much stuck to our usual routines. Mia went to class and I went to work, but in the evenings she would have a hot dinner waiting for me and we would sit down and eat together. I even got her to laugh a few times.

After dinner we watched TV, read or just talked. A lot of times Mia would study while I sat in the living room just to be in her presence. I had already told Brice that he had to respect me and not come by my apartment and make a scene. Miraculously, he stayed away. My love for Mia grew stronger.

After that first night, Mia got the bed and I slept on the pull-out sofa. That was the arrangement. No climbing into bed with me in the middle of the night. I broke it down to Mia. I told her that as much as I wanted to comfort her, I was a hot-blooded male and couldn't take her lying next to me with her body pressed up against mine without having certain feelings and desires. That one night when she came to me, I lay awake all night long holding her in my arms until she fell asleep. I stared at the ceiling all night. I had my arms around her waist and my hands on her flat stomach. She felt so warm with her legs and butt pressed against mine. Mia looked so peaceful, with no cares in the world.

On my desk at work I keep a few photos of my moms, myself

and Brice when we were younger and some basic-training photos. I also have a few photos of Brice, Mia and myself together. I was sitting there late one evening trying to catch up on some paperwork, but I couldn't really concentrate. I had too much on my mind. I kept picturing Mia back at my apartment. She was such a beautiful woman. I had already called her and told her that I would be late. She said that she would wait up for me and keep my dinner warm. That made me smile. Mia made me smile.

There is this one picture of Mia that I had snapped: She is seated, looking like a sweet angel. She has this sensual, half-smile expression on her face, and she's looking straight into the camera like she is looking straight into my soul. For once, her hair is in loose curls framing her face. In that photo, which I look at often, she looks so peaceful and happy. Then there's this photo that somebody snapped of the three of us. Mia is in the middle with her arms around Brice and myself and she has this huge smile on her face like she's having the time of her life. Those are my favorite pictures of her. Sometimes, when everyone else has left for the day, I can sit there and just look at those pictures, trying to figure her out and understand the mess my life is in.

And that is exactly how Sergeant Blackwell found me, staring at the photo of Mia. He had forgotten his keys and came back to retrieve them. He was the closest person that I could call a friend other than Christian. Blackwell was in his fifties and was a born-again Christian. The man was deep. He had it together both mentally and spiritually. I think he saw me as a son or something. I used to go to his house for Sunday dinner until he started preaching to me about my sinful ways. He didn't mean any harm, but I wasn't ready to change. I respected him. He was a good and decent man.

"You still here?" he asked as he rummaged through his desk drawer.

He had seen me quickly put the picture back onto my desk, but he acted as if he hadn't seen it.

"Is Mia still staying with you?"

I nodded.

"Christian, I know it's none of my business, but, man, sooner or later you are going to have to confront and conquer your demons. You can't run from the truth because when everything is said and done, that is all you have."

I opened my mouth to respond.

"You don't have to say anything. I know what I see in front of me, and you aren't happy. The only time I see a twinkle in your eyes is when you are talking about Mia or when you are in her presence. Life isn't fair, but we don't have to idly sit back and let it control us. Take charge of your destiny, man. The truth hurts, but you have to stand up and be a man. Tell her. That's the least you can do. The truth will set you free." With those words, he retrieved his keys and walked out the door.

I picked the photo of Mia back up, held it to my heart and thought about the meaning behind what Blackwell had just told me. I had some major decisions to make.

Like I said, when I came home for lunch on Friday around noon, Brice was at the apartment and Mia was packing her few items of clothing. Mia and Brice thanked me for everything and they left hand in hand. I dropped down on the sofa and shook my head in disbelief.

I must admit, it was lonely coming home to my apartment that evening. Mia couldn't help but put her signature and stamp on everything she touched. In just a week, she had turned my house into a home. I guess she needed some kind of distraction to keep her mind off her problems, so she'd taken it upon herself to redecorate my bachelor pad, as she called it. She said she was going to give it a woman's touch.

I have thought a lot about what Mia said about making choices and what would happen if I had to choose. I honestly don't know the answer to that question. I know I definitely didn't like the shit that Brice was putting her through. I had tried to talk to my man, but he didn't know why he kept messing up. Personally, I thought that someone, mainly Brice, was going to have to get help or something serious was going to happen. I mean, this couldn't keep going on like it was. Fights, apologies, get back together, fuck and the cycle repeated itself. Something had to give. They were like two time bombs waiting to explode. I guess something, some major drama, was bound to happen sooner or later. Sooner came before later.

I couldn't avoid Brice forever, and I felt as if I had overstayed my welcome at Christian's. The only thing left to do was to go home to my husband or go home to Mama. I ended up back with Brice after he literally begged and cried for me to come home. That was the most humble I had ever seen my husband. He actually got down on his knees in front of me as I sat on Christian's sofa and cried and begged. Brice said that he would seek help and go to counseling with me. He'd do anything, even go to anger-management classes. It worked, because I'm back home. I told him, "Let it happen one more time and I'm gone." I mean it this time. Really I do. Do you think I enjoy getting my butt beat? Hell, no.

I am counting down the last days of classes. I will have my bachelor's degree in two months. God, if you can hear me, please don't let anything happen. I will have realized at least one of my dreams. I can hardly wait, and Mama is so proud. She once told me to never rely on a man for everything. Never let a man become your whole life because then you lose yourself; always have something that you can fall back on. She said, "God rest his soul, as much as I loved him, that is what I did with your Daddy. I lost my identity somewhere. And after he was gone, it completely destroyed me."

Brice, surprisingly, is really excited for me as well. He has our entire day planned. He is taking me out dancing, dinner and the works. Maybe he is changing. Things are okay with us, not great, but at least okay. We are not walking around each other like strangers, and we even had our first counseling session. Brice admitted that he has this fear of losing me. For the first time, I saw this vulnerable side of him.

At school, Malcolm is seriously sweating me. We have a class together now, so I have to see him every day, but he is making it hard
because there is definitely an attraction between the two of us. Malcolm has this sex appeal thing going on, and he knows it. And that
dark skin and bald head. Ohhh, so sexy.

Sometimes we study together in between classes at the library
and we'll talk about stuff. He can be really deep sometimes. He un-
derstands what I'm going through. Sometimes I feel that Brice can't
understand because he has already gone through what I'm dealing
with now. It's hard starting out in the world and being unsure of
yourself and your abilities. I want to make my mark on the world;
Malcolm, he can understand all that because he is where I am.

This morning, I approached the new day with a new attitude.
When I got up, Brice had already left for work. I showered, got
dressed and actually let my hair down, literally. I usually wear my
thick hair pulled back in a ponytail. But today I felt giddy, so I hot-
curled some soft, loose curls into my hair and put on a denim dress.
I met Malcolm at our usual place, on the fifth floor in a study room,
at the newly renovated library. He was already there, with his head
buried in a book. We had a test coming up soon, so he was getting
a head start. I was beginning to realize that behind Malcolm's rough,
macho exterior, he was all right. And too sexy for his and my own
good.

Malcolm did a double take, which he tried to play off, when I
entered the room and closed the door. I don't think he had ever seen
me with my hair down or me in anything other than jeans, T-shirts
and caps. Brice hated for me to wear caps when I was with him, but
he didn't complain when I wore them to school. I guess he figured
the more unattractive I was, the better. Today I even had on a touch
of bright red lip gloss. Red is my favorite color.

"I see you made it. I was beginning to think that you had stood
me up," he said as he looked up with a smile on his sexy lips and
looked back down into his open textbook.

"Yeah, I'm running late because my question to the professor took longer than I thought. You know how he has to go around the world and back to explain everything."

We both laughed at that as I pulled out my own book to begin reading chapters twenty-three and twenty-four. We had a test coming up within a few days. I glanced up later to find Malcolm staring at me.

"What?"

"What do you mean?"

"Why are you staring at me?"

"I'm just admiring your beauty. You are such a pretty lady, Mia."

"Am I?"

"Oh, come on, Mia, you know you're pretty."

"Yeah, there's me and tons of other pretty faces on campus."

"I'm not talking about them. I'm talking about you. Anyway, you are different. You're special."

"Yeah right. I bet you say that to all your friends," I said, blushing.

"You are, Mia, and no, I don't tell everyone that. You don't give yourself enough credit."

Malcolm continued to stare at me with just a little lust in his eyes. It was no secret that he wanted to get with me. He had told me enough times, but he knew the deal. I'm not going to lie. Malcolm had it going on. I had imagined, many times, what it would be like to feel him inside me as he kissed me with those juicy lips. I knew it would be so gooood. But I wanted him as a friend, and I was starting to enjoy the time and conversations that we had together. I didn't see Christian as much anymore, so I needed someone.

"Malcolm, why are you still staring at me?" I asked as I smiled at him. "You're making me nervous."

"Why do you stay with him?"

"Stay with who?"

"Come on, Mia, you know who I'm talking about."

"Why do you think?"

"I don't know. That's why I'm asking. Enlighten me."

"He's my husband and I love him."

"Explain to me how you can love someone who doesn't support your college career and who uses your face as a punching bag," he said in an accusing voice.

"You don't know what my life is like, Malcolm. Don't pretend to know until you have walked in my shoes."

"Oh come on, Mia. I have heard the rumors and I've seen the bruises on you myself after he has laid down the law. I've seen your hand in a cast because of him. Be for real."

"Well, since you know, there have been only a few episodes since we've been married. Most of the time, we are just like any other married couple. He loves me and I love him. Case closed. You don't see the times that he brings me flowers just because or surprises me with a bottle of my favorite perfume. You don't see when he calls me in the middle of the day to say I love you. You don't see any of that. And he's getting excited about my graduation. My uncle Larry told me that marriage is hard work. There are going to be ups and downs. I can't throw in the towel just like that."

"I don't think your uncle Larry was referring to your sticking around and getting your ass beat."

I just looked at him as I felt my good feeling leaving and my day going straight to hell.

"Mia, I'm sorry, but I don't see how your husband, or any man for that matter, can hurt you. When I look at you, I just want to hold you and protect you. I don't understand how Sergeant Matthew can use his hands to hit you and then turn around and use those same hands to bring you pleasure."

I didn't say anything. I sat there, unmoving.

"How can you continue on? Do you just forgive and forget and spread your legs whenever he wants you to?"

"Yeah, that's right, I forgive, and I almost, just almost, forget when things are going great for months. What do you suggest, Malcolm?" I asked as I found myself getting upset. "Should I sleep with you, get a good fuck from the stud on campus, and then all my problems will be solved?"

"That'll work. No, I'm kidding, Mia."

"It's not that simple. Life is much more complicated," I stated.

"Let's just drop it. Okay? I see I'm upsetting you. I have just one more comment and then I'm going to leave it alone. It's true what they say. If he hits you once, he'll hit you again. It's not going to stop. I've seen it before in my own family. You are his property. You belong to him. I've seen how possessive he is of you. It's his way or no way. One of my uncles used to beat his wife whenever he got drunk, which was practically every Friday night. It finally stopped when she shot him to death. Believe me, it's not going to stop."

Malcolm was the catalyst for the end of life as I know it. I should have just stayed away from him. But you know me, always the flirt who can take care of herself until the heat gets too hot. Well, it got real hot. I was playing with fire, and if you play with fire too long, eventually you get burned.

It was about five weeks after the club incident. Brice had gone out of town for a few days, and I decided that I was going to go out with the gang. I knew that I had Christian to cover for me. I deserved it. I would graduate soon, and I wanted to celebrate. So Carolyn, Tiffany, Malcolm and I had all gone to this nonmilitary club to dance, drink and have a good time. It was just like the last time.

Malcolm knew that I couldn't handle my liquor and normally didn't drink, but tonight he kept refilling my glass. I even had my first shot of bourbon. I was feeling too good. Before I knew it, I was out of it and he was taking me home. Once we got to my apartment, he walked me up the stairs, unlocked the door for me and waltzed on in behind me, playfully rubbing my ass through my pants. I just giggled as I slightly stumbled. He knew that Brice was out of town.

By now I was feeling good, with no inhibitions. Malcolm asked if we had anything to drink as he made himself at home in my refrigerator. I had gone to the bathroom to relieve myself, and when I came back he was sitting on the sofa with the TV on and remote in hand like he was staying for a while. Like he owned the place.

"Come here, Mia," he said as he held out his right hand with this lustful look in his eyes.

I walked slowly over to him and stood above him at the sofa.

"I don't bite," he said as he pulled me down onto the sofa and on top of him.

"Listen, Malcolm, maybe this isn't such a good idea. Maybe you should go." I could feel his hardness through his pants as his hands massaged my back. My nipples were standing at attention.

"Chill, baby. Just sit down and we can watch some TV. Don't freak out on me."

We sat there for a while watching some off-the-wall movie. Malcolm laughed every now and then. Out of nowhere, Malcolm leaned over, turned my face to his and kissed me. The kiss was full of passion, tongue and desire. I felt that kiss all the way down to my toes. I knew there was no turning back. I wanted him. I wanted him bad. I could smell the sexual energy seeping out of his pores.

"Wait right here. Let me change into something more comfortable." Then I started laughing because that was so cliché, and I had always wanted to say that.

He said, "I'll be right here, baby. I'm not going anywhere. I got something for you."

I went into my bedroom and changed into this short black silky number that Brice had purchased for me from Victoria's Secret. Or was it Frederick's of Hollywood? It left little to the imagination. That's funny, because when I was in public he didn't want me to show any skin, yet when he fucked me he wanted me to look like a whore.

When I walked back into the living room Malcolm's eyes almost fell out of his head.

"Damn. Come here, girl. You need to stop covering up all this at school, baby," he said as he fondled my breasts through my negligee, and chills went up and down my spine.

I did as he said and sat down on the sofa next to him. As he kissed and licked my neck, my legs voluntarily spread, open and waiting.

Malcolm had pulled off his shirt, and I ran my hands across his toned chocolate chest and his tattoo as we kissed. By now he had pulled the spaghetti straps of my black negligee down to expose my breasts and erect nipples. He was squeezing and fondling them as I lifted my chest to meet him and his eager tongue. As his hand urgently caressed my body, from my stomach to my thighs, his other hand was pulling down my gown and panties in one pull. Shivers were running up and down my arms.

Malcolm stopped. He stopped touching me. Malcolm stopped those wonderful sensations. As I sat there butt naked in all my glory, he reclined on the floor and admired me . . . from a distance.

"Tell me you want me."

"What?"

"You heard me. Tell me you want to feel me inside you."

"Come on. You know I do."

"I want to hear you say it, baby. All this time, you haven't let me get any. I want to hear you say it."

I didn't say anything. I tried to pull him closer. Malcolm wouldn't budge. He sat there on the floor with a slight smirk on his face as he stroked his jimmy, which had made an appearance, from his unzipped pants. Thick, long and black.

"Don't get shy now. Don't you want to feel this?"

I nodded my head.

"You think you can handle all this?" he asked as he stood within inches of my face. Malcolm laughed and bent down as he kissed me passionately.

As Malcolm massaged between my thighs, he stuck a finger in. Then another. When the man got on his hands and knees, pulled me to the edge of the couch and placed his face between my spread legs and went down, all I could do was throw my head back, close my eyes and grab that bald head and hold on for dear life. I had never felt that good in my entire life. My body was on fire. He was hitting the spot. Shit! He was hitting it just right. Like he owned my stuff!

At right about that moment, there was a knock at the door. He stopped. "No, don't stop, baby." I stopped moaning, and we both stared at the door, silently willing the person on the other side to go away so that we could finish. Whoever was knocking kept knocking and was not giving up and going away. Suddenly I heard a key going in the lock. Then the door swung wide open and Christian walked in and grabbed Malcolm off of me. Everything after that happened in slow motion, in a daze. I remember screaming and Malcolm trying to get his shirt on and pants up, and Christian yelling, screaming at me to get dressed and me running, totally humiliated, down the hallway.

Then everything was quiet. Dead silence. I heard some low conversation, angry voices. I heard a door slam hard, and then Christian was in there sitting on the bed by me and I had the sheet pulled up to cover my nakedness. Christian looked at me and I looked at him for a few seconds.

"What in the hell was that, Mia? Just what in the hell were you doing? Do you really want Brice to beat your ass again?" he screamed at me.

Suddenly I went off. "Leave me alone, dammit. You are not my keeper. You are just like Brice. Stay the fuck away from me. I don't need you to make my life miserable too."

The affects of the alcohol were all but gone, and I was very clear-headed and realized what I had done or almost done. I had almost had sex with a man who wasn't my husband. By now I was softly crying out of humiliation and also because I had never seen this side of Christian, much less talked to him in that manner. I couldn't speak or even look at him now. I pulled the sheet up tighter around me. I felt so exposed.

Christian finally realized what he was doing and how he was acting. He leaned over and held me in his arms while I continued crying.

"Mia, I know it has been rough for you lately, but you aren't like this . . . You don't sleep around and cheat on your husband . . . even if Brice has given you reason to."

"Oh, Christian, I don't know . . . what happened. I needed to feel loved, and Malcolm was showing me that."

Christian stared at me in disbelief. "Malcolm just wanted to get in your pants. Nothing more, nothing less."

"Are you disappointed in me?"

He didn't respond.

"I need for you not to lose respect for me. It means a lot to me. You mean a lot to me."

"I would never do that," he stated with sincere honesty.

For some reason, with that revelation, I felt this strong urge to kiss him and feel closer to him. I leaned up and kissed him softly on his lips. Our lips parted, and I felt his hesitant tongue as it explored the inside of my mouth. He paused for a moment. Then he was into the kiss, and I lowered the sheet and placed his hands on my exposed breasts. We kissed passionately and he touched, squeezed me in places and then . . . he grabbed me by the wrists and pushed me roughly away.

"Damn, Mia. You know I can't do this! You know this can't happen. Listen, I'm outta here. Get yourself together before . . . just get your act together and stop behaving like a child and start behaving like the lady you are," he said as he rose to walk out of the bedroom without even looking at me.

I screamed and cried. "Christian, I'm sorry. Are you going to tell Brice?"

He kept walking.

"Christian, are you telling him? You know what will happen if he finds out. Pleassse don't tell. You've got to promise me this will remain between us."

He stopped at the doorway, turned around and finally looked me dead in the eyes.

"Mia, I'm not going to tell him about any of this. I'm going to blame this on the alcohol that you've consumed. You aren't thinking or acting rationally right now. Neither am I. I'm going to pretend like this never happened. You do the same."

I laid back on the bed with a sigh of relief and said, "Okay."

Right before Christian walked out the door, I asked him, "What if I had met you that summer at the cookout? It could have all been so different."

"But you didn't. You met my best friend."

Christian walked up the hallway and out the door. I lay there for the rest of the night, relived his kiss and the feel of his hands as they touched my body in intimate places. And I thought about what he had said. Funny, I didn't even think about Malcolm. Christian invaded my thoughts.

They say there is always quiet before the storm. That was definitely true in our case. I avoided Mia and Brice for as long as I could, and it was a bit strange with Mia when I eventually saw her again. I still couldn't get her kiss or the feel of her body out of my head, and the guilt was eating me up.

At first there were a lot of silences, no eye contact or being alone with each other for us. Then I guess we realized how foolish we were acting because soon we were as before. Well, I can't say exactly as before, because there is never any turning back or going back to the way things were. The kiss and the touch happened, sparks flew, and that couldn't be forgotten. Life is really funny like that. For every action there is a consequence to deal with. You have to lie in the bed you make.

Mia told me that she didn't have any more problems with Malcolm. I learned later that was far from the truth. Even though I don't think that I walked in on any problems in the first place. It looked like they were both about to get their grooves on. But I made it absolutely clear to him who Mia's husband was, who I was and what we could do to his flourishing military career. I advised Mr. Malcolm to keep his dick in his pants when it came to Mia. He could screw anybody else he wanted to, just not Mia. He got the picture loud and clear. I hated playing hardball, but I had to do what I had to do.

Hell, in my younger days, I probably would have done the same thing. Shit, yeah. I would have tried to get in the panties of someone who looked like Mia.

32 Mia

After Christian kicked Malcolm out of my apartment, I thought that Malcolm would have avoided me like the plague. I knew that I would if the situation had been reversed, but that didn't happen. It was like Malcolm got a thrill out of pursuing me even more. I for one knew that I was skating on very thin ice and was just lucky that Christian promised not to tell Brice what he had witnessed.

I just wanted Malcolm to leave me the hell alone while I was still on top. Malcolm, on the other hand, had very different plans. The fool wouldn't leave me alone. If it hadn't been such a sad situation, it actually would have been funny. I could really pick them. I thought that he would get the message when I ignored him in class, which probably wasn't the smartest thing to do, but Malcolm wasn't deterred. That night was a drunken moment of weakness. He knew I didn't want to sleep with him. Or maybe I did, just to "show" Brice. I don't know.

I had gone back to class that following Monday, and instead of sitting over near the wall by Malcolm, as I usually did, I sat at a desk in the back corner of the classroom. When I walked in just before class started, Malcolm was already seated in our usual spot. I saw him glance at me and try to make eye contact, but I walked to the back of the room and sat at a desk between two girls. I noticed him looking back at me throughout the lecture, but I pretended not to notice and kept taking notes.

I had glanced at him a few times when he didn't notice and he seemed to be fine. He didn't have any circles under his eyes, unlike me who hadn't slept a wink, and he didn't seem to be upset. Malcolm looked as fine as usual. Even in shorts and a T-shirt, the man had it going on. For a brief moment, my mind drifted back to that night and what could have happened. After class, I fumbled with my book bag and stayed behind to ask the professor a question, hoping the entire time that Malcolm would take that as a hint and go on without me. When I finally walked out of the classroom, I didn't see him, but before I could make it down the hallway, Malcolm was at my side.

"Mia, what's going on? What's up with the cold shoulder?"

I glanced over at him and kept walking. "What do you mean?"

"Don't give me that bullshit. You know exactly what I mean."

"My husband, remember him, my husband's best friend walks in on us about to have sex and you ask me what's wrong?"

"Listen, baby, we can go to a hotel or somewhere next time."

I actually stopped and looked at him in utter amazement.

"Are you crazy? You know Brice and what he is capable of. Believe me, there won't be a next time."

Malcolm grabbed my elbow and led me over near the wall away from the hall traffic.

"Oh, so you are going to dis me now? It's like that? Is that the little game you play, Mia? You weren't screaming all that bullshit the other night. You were too busy moaning and groaning while I went down on you."

I pulled away from him with no response. The look I gave him said it all. Malcolm pushed me back against the wall. "Is that how you like to be handled, Mia? Maybe you get off on being manhandled. Is that what makes you come, Mia? You know I almost fell for your little innocent, wronged wife act, but you are nothing more than a tease who likes some dick on the side. I can't believe I told you all that stuff about my family and my uncle."

"Let go of me, Malcolm. Leave me alone," I said as I pulled away from him. "I thought that you were my friend. I thought that we had something in common. I thought you understood. I thought you knew me. If you were a friend, you'd leave me alone."

Malcolm ran to catch up with me. "Look, I'm sorry. I didn't mean those things I said. I like you, Mia, and I just wanted the chance to finish what we started. Don't close me out like this. You're just afraid that he's going to find out. He won't. You said yourself that you trust Christian," he said as he pulled me to him once again.

"Malcolm, stop before someone sees us."

"You felt and tasted so good the other night. I can't wait to be with you again. Don't worry. He won't find out."

"I told you that there isn't going to be a next time. What do I have to do to make you understand?"

By now we had made it to a corner where the long hallway intercepted a narrow hallway where the professors' offices were. Malcolm pulled me into a private corner.

"Baby, don't play me like this. I need you. I want you. I don't know what games you're playing . . ."

I managed to free myself when a professor walked out of his office. As I ran down the hallway and looked back at Malcolm, I knew that I hadn't heard or seen the last of him. Stupid, stupid, stupid. I was so stupid. I ran from Brice and straight into the arms of another man who was just like him. One who didn't respect women and thought of them only as sex objects. I told him all my secrets . . . I was so wrong, as usual.

Brice returned from his trip, none the wiser, and he was willing to continue the counseling with Mia and take it seriously. He told me that he didn't know what happened, but he realized that life is too short and it isn't every day that you meet the lady that you want to spend the rest of your life with. He felt like Mia was his true soul mate regardless of the problems that they had had in the past, and he wanted to save what was left of their marriage. Mia was elated from what he told me. Yeah, things were taking a turn in their marriage . . . for the better. But shit always has a way of catching up with you. Usually when you least expect it. What's done in the dark will come to light sooner or later.

Mia graduated with her bachelor's degree in education. We all attended the graduation and screamed and cheered for our girl. We were probably as excited as she was, and believe me, she was ecstatic. Mia strutted across that stage in her black cap and gown and shook hands with the president of the college with such grace and a smile that could light up the night. It was a thousand-watt smile. Her mother shed tears of joy, saying how proud her father would have been. If only she knew what her daughter had to go through to get that piece of paper. Mia stayed focused, somehow, through all that drama over the years with Brice.

Afterwards, we all went out to this trendy seafood restaurant, the Fayetteville Fish Market, and had a leisurely lunch, and later that evening, we danced the night away. My date was a lady named Vicki, whom I had met weeks earlier. Yeah, I was still trying to ease back into the dating arena. The truth would have to stay buried. In the earlier part of the evening I could have sworn that Mia was treating her cold, and I could sense some jealousy, but maybe it was my imagination. You can never tell about women. Mia was no different.

It was Mia's day and she was in true form. She and Brice reminded me of how they had acted when they were first married. They were feeding each other and all over each other. They couldn't get enough of each other, and I actually saw love reflected in Mia's eyes. In the past it had been fear that I saw. It is a day and time that I will never forget for as long as I live because it was the last time that we were together as a unit. We were happy, smiling and full of laughter and joy. If someone could have snapped a photo of us and froze that place in time, they would have never imagined what would go down a few weeks later. I know I didn't.

Malcolm had a reputation as being a hell-raiser for good reason. I guess his image and reputation were more important than his military career, because he started bragging and telling anyone who would listen what he had done to Sergeant Matthew's wife. He was telling everyone how she was love starved, how she was a freak, how he took her in her own house and how she was ready and willing to open wide. I also learned much later that Malcolm had been harassing Mia at the university. He would approach her between classes, telling her how he couldn't wait to taste her again. He was obsessed and wouldn't leave her alone or take no for an answer.

Anyway, it didn't take long for word to spread, especially on a military base. So before I could do damage control, Brice got wind of it around the same time that I did. Something told me to get over to their apartment as soon as I could. I had this feeling, this intuition, that all hell was about to break loose. How right I was. Hell had busted wide open!

When I arrived at their apartment, I heard Brice before I saw him. I'm sure everyone in the building heard him. As I quickly made my way up the stairway, two steps at a time, I could hear him screaming at Mia and calling her every name in the book and some names that weren't.

I made it halfway through the doorway.

"Hey, man, take it easy," I said to a very angry Brice, who had Mia cornered near the half-open door. Her lip was swollen and bleeding, her button-down shirt was torn at the sleeve and there was a handprint on her left cheek. He had hit her hard enough to leave his print, his stamp.

"Christian, you stay the hell out of this, man. I'm going to kill this bitch. She has fucked some punk on base. She let him fuck her; she actually let him go up in her."

Mia was crying, "Brice, I didn't screw him. He's lying. You have to believe me. I love you, baby." He responded by slapping her again. Brice was so mad that his facial features were distorted. He wasn't holding back, either. It was obvious that he wanted to do some serious damage to Mia. Brice wasn't taking any prisoners. He wanted to draw blood and teach her a lesson. A lesson she would not soon forget. I wasn't going to let him hit her again.

"You love me . . . you don't love me!" he screamed into her bruised face. "If you loved me, you wouldn't have betrayed me like this!"

"Listen, man, I heard, but let's discuss this like civilized people. It's not going to solve anything to beat her ass again." By now he had grabbed Mia's arm and was twisting it behind her back.

"I don't have anything to say to this . . . this . . . whore."

Mia was screaming now like he was killing her, or soon would, and her screaming was only making him angrier.

I had inched my way a little closer. Brice had Mia up against the wall with his hand enclosed halfway around her neck.

"Why, Mia. Why?" he asked as he caressed her face, then suddenly banged her head against the wall. "I love you. I'd give up my life for you. Why? Just tell me why."

I was thinking that he was going to choke her to death or beat her brains out, so I tackled him to the floor and gave Mia a chance to get out of his reach.

"Man, get the fuck off me! Let me handle my business."

"Get your ass back over here, Mia," and he lunged for her as he attempted to break away from my grip.

Mia was scared as hell. She turned to run, and he grabbed her shirttail, and she was screaming and crying, and Brice was screaming and cursing, and a crowd had started to gather, and then . . . the shirt tore . . . I can still hear the sound of her white cotton shirt ripping . . . and Mia fell headfirst down the flight of stairs. I didn't even realize it was me screaming, "No! My God, no!" until I reached the bottom of the stairs and lifted her head up onto my lap. Mia was unconscious, limp, and blood was quickly spreading from a wound on the back of her head.

Brice made his way slowly down the stairs as if he were in a drunken daze. The man was crying and disoriented. He tried to get to Mia when he saw what he had done.

"Muthafucka, is this what you wanted? Are you happy now? Stay the fuck away from her! You made her run into the arms of another man. You cold-blooded son of a bitch. You don't even deserve her, man. You don't even deserve her," I screamed as I laid my head down on top of Mia and cried.

"Mia, wake up, baby. You're going to be okay. You are safe with me now. I love you. You can't leave me now. I promise he won't hurt you again. Just wake up, baby. Wake up."

My emotional outburst stopped Brice dead in his tracks for a few seconds, and he reeled back in complete shock and surprise before recovering and fully understanding the implications of what I had said.

"Get away from my wife. I trusted you, man. I can't believe this shit. You goddamn muthafucka, I trusted you," he screamed as he lunged for me.

I don't remember much more except for someone in the crowd restraining him before he tried to beat me to death. At that point, he could have done anything to me because I didn't have the strength to move, much less defend myself. I vaguely remember hearing the siren from the ambulance in the distance, as it got closer and closer. I can barely recall them prying me away from Mia so that they could take her limp body away. I remember looking up and seeing shadows of people huddled together, whispering, with solemn looks on their faces. The last thing I remember was looking up and seeing the cold, heartless stare that Brice gave me and hearing his last words echoing over and over as I walked slowly out of that apartment for the last time. *I trusted you, man.*

34 Mia

I guess my black knight in shining armor turned into a frog, huh? Don't let anyone tell you that fairy tales do come true because that would be a lie. I was so stupid, so naive, but never again. Never again! I guess you say I got what I deserved. Hell, no, I didn't. I deserved so much more. What fool marries someone after only knowing that person for a month? The answer to that question is a fool in love. A person who found true love for the first time in her life and wanted to hold on to it and never lose it.

You know, I've been thinking a lot. I've been in this hospital bed for two days now with nothing but time on my hands. I'm going to stop blaming myself. I didn't do anything wrong. For the longest time, I blamed myself. I kept trying to break down and analyze everything in our relationship to determine what went wrong, to see what I did wrong. Maybe I could have done things differently, maybe I could have been more understanding, maybe I should have had the baby that he wanted so badly . . . The reality is that my husband, or soon-to-be ex-husband, has some serious problems that he needs to deal with. I can't help him with those issues. He has to resolve them himself. That is something that he has to do alone. All I can do is take pleasure in the fact that I did everything that I could do, and I loved, loved him with all my heart and soul from beginning to the bitter end. That's a fact. That will never change. But I'm not about to stay in a relationship and die for love. I know that much.

Christian, what can I say about my dear, darling Christian? He has been heaven sent as usual. That man is too good to be true. I would trust him with my life. He has been here for me every day and every night, trying to cheer me up and provide some form of comfort. I always feel safe and secure in his presence. I took a pretty bad fall. They thought that I had a concussion. But I am mending physically, at least. I am in here for observational purposes only. Christian has been the only person besides the doctors and nurses that I have seen. I asked them not to let Brice into my room under any circumstances. He has sent flowers and apologies every day. That's too little too late. I didn't press charges because I want to go on with my life and forget the past, and Brice is the past. But it will be so hard to forget Brice.

Anyway, back to Christian. I woke up last night to find him sitting in the recliner in my room. He had a blanket wrapped around him and he was sitting there watching me sleep. It looked like he had been there for a while. Christian is so tired and mentally stressed out that it is written all over his face. The man loves me and I know that I feel something, strong emotions, for him. Yeah, he finally told me what I knew all along but didn't want to admit to myself. Christian told me that he loved me and had loved me for a long time, but he knew that nothing could ever come of it because of Brice. I didn't say anything because I didn't know what to say or what to feel. I don't feel anything anymore. I am numb both physically and emotionally. What can I say? Brice broke my heart. Broke my heart into tiny little pieces and then stomped all over them.

Christian is in so much pain. This is the first time in his life that he hasn't had Brice in his corner for support. He made a choice and he chose me. Christian said that he had to stand up, be a man and do the right thing.

So, I lie here today with Christian somewhere buying me a magazine to read. As I finger his mother's beautiful cross that I wear around my neck, I thank God for him. I have so many decisions to make about my future. Is my marriage over? Hell yeah, in its present form. Do I still love the man? I hate to admit it, but I do. Is there hope for Christian in my life as a possible lover? I don't know. He is or was so close to Brice that they are almost inseparable in my mind. But I admit that I care for and possibly love him. Maybe I'll make a clean cut and go on with my life. I mean, I'm still young. I finally got my bachelor's degree and can teach now.

Christian has asked me to come home to him when they release me, but I have to get away from here, away from them. He is going to drive me home to Mama when they release me, which will probably be tomorrow. And then I have the huge task of deciding what to do with the rest of my life. Who knows what my future holds? Only time will tell. Lord knows I don't have any idea.

I fucked up big-time this time. It was only a matter of time before I self-destructed. I have sat here in this apartment the last couple of days with all these reminders of Mia around me and I realize what a fool I have been. That's a little late though. Mia doesn't want to see me or have anything to do with me. And you know what . . . I can't blame her.

I did something last night that I haven't done in years. I went to church and prayed. I went into the brick church on Main Street, went to the front pew, knelt down and I prayed. Prayed and cried for all the mistakes I made with Mia. I prayed that she would find it in her heart to forgive me, and I prayed that I could start liking myself again. Afterwards, I got up and sat, thinking and staring into space for what seemed like hours.

I don't know what happened that night. Hell, I do know. As usual, I let my temper get the best of me. But I swear before God that I didn't mean for Mia to fall down those stairs. I know Christian and Mia don't believe me, but it is the God honest truth. I wanted to hurt her like she had hurt my heart, but I didn't want her to end up in the hospital.

I realize now that I drove her into his arms. I understand that she didn't actually sleep with him. That is some consolation for me. There was a day when I would have done the same thing. You know, you see a pretty lady having problems with the old man, so you make your move to comfort her and you end up in her bed.

Christian. I have seen him from a distance on base, but I haven't talked with him since the day after the incident. I don't trust myself to talk to him. I want to rip his heart out. It's weird not being able to call him up and just talk. I feel like I should be crying on his shoulder about this shit with Mia, but he's part of it. My best friend is in love with my woman. *My wife!* Ain't that some messed up shit? Of all the people in the entire universe, I thought—no, I knew—that I could trust him. But he told me, he looked me in the eye, and told me that he loves Mia. I admit it took a lot for him to do what he did and to tell me that, but my heart is cold when it comes to him. Hell, I can't say that either. I don't know what I feel anymore.

Mia. I know I have lost her for good. I can't even think of life without her. So I am not going to give up. I am not going to let her give up on us. I will get help. Go to therapy, do whatever it takes to win her back. I know that this is something that I have to do for myself, not just for her. But I want her back if she will have me. I have never stopped loving her and never will. Mia is my African princess, my woman, my soul mate, my heart. It will take some time, but time is all I have now. My first stop will be resolving some issues with my father. Yeah, that's definitely the first stop.

Christian and I have had a lifetime of friendship and love. I don't know . . . my brotha betrayed me with my wife. No, he didn't sleep with her or even make a move on her. In fact, he was the good friend that she needed when I was putting her through all those changes. But for Christian to lust after my wife, not just some man's wife on the street, but me, his brotha. I don't know . . .

Like I said before, I have all the time in the world. I have to take one day at a time. Everything will work out. It always does for me.

36   Christian

Sometimes you have to stand up and be a man. You have to make a decision that is going to affect the rest of your life. Well, I've done that, and I am proud of myself and I know Moms would have been proud of me too, even though my life is in total shambles now.

I finally told Mia that I love her. She didn't say much and the earth didn't shake, but that's fine because I know that she has been through hell. The main thing is that she didn't turn me away or ask me to leave. I get my reward when she smiles for just a second, and the smile is all for me. I honestly don't know what, if anything, will happen with me and Mia. It hurts, it hurts like hell. I don't know what I expected from her . . . to run into my open arms . . . I don't know. But regardless, I was true to my heart for the first time in my life.

I'm driving Mia home to her mom's after she's discharged from the hospital. She declined my offer to stay with me. I guess that's for the best, because that would be an awkward situation. During the drive home we will have plenty of time to talk. When I stay with her at the hospital, she talks about everything and everybody but Brice. She is doing some serious hurting. Her heart is wide-open.

Speaking of Brice, I've seen him from a distance on base, and I could feel the hate. I don't blame him, though. It's not every day that your best friend, ex-best friend, admits that he is in love with your wife. I know at some point we will have to sit down and talk. We owe each other that much. That point will come in time. I may have lost the only family and brother that I ever had or ever will have in life.

Mia. I love her. Hell, I am not going to lie. I love her with all my heart and soul. I would love to have her in my life, but it is all so complicated. The ties that bind. The ties that bind have probably already been severed in my case. I have already given up everything for her, and I still don't get the girl. That's a trip. Life's a trip.

Mia came into my life and unfroze a frozen heart. Mia, the lady with the beautiful smile. I know that she feels something for me. I can see it in her eyes, and the eyes don't lie. "They are the window into the soul," is what Moms used to tell me all the time. Time will tell. I don't intend to give up. For the first time in my life, I believe in something . . . love.

"God never gives us more than we can handle" is what Mama is always telling me. Well, he has definitely given me my limit because I can't take any more. I'm maxed out! I'm overdrawn! I am surviving one day at a time. Just one day at a time. I can't do any better than that right now.

I'm home, recuperating, with Mama for now. Christian drove me here straight from my discharge from the hospital. I couldn't bear to go back to that apartment for even a moment. It holds too many memories, both good and bad. A lot of things were said on that long drive home. Mama has been pampering me so much that it is almost disgusting. Who am I kidding—I could almost get used to this if it weren't for the circumstances. I still have my good days, though they are far and few in between, and my bad days. Many nights I wake up trembling from nightmares in which Brice is towering over me. Sometimes I start crying and can't stop, and other days when I'm feeling strong, I realize that I'll get past this. Life goes on, and this too shall pass.

I haven't seen Brice since the "incident." That's how I refer to what happened. After I left him, Brice drove down one evening, knocked and banged on the door, and begged and pleaded with me to talk with him, but Mama informed him she'd call the police if he didn't leave me alone and get off her property. I stayed upstairs, like a coward, hiding out in my old bedroom the entire time until he left. As he returned to his car, I pulled back the curtain and looked out the window. He looked up at that instant and our eyes met for a brief second. With a pounding heart, I quickly closed the curtain on the window and him. After that, he called several times declaring his undying love, telling me how much he missed me, how he wanted to be with me and how we could make it work if I gave him another chance. He promised that he would never, ever, hit me again. And get this, Brice said he forgave me for messing around with Malcolm. Each time our conversation ended with me in tears. I'm like an open wound. I'm totally raw when it comes to him. I'm not strong enough emotionally to face him yet. Finally, Mama told him to deal with her as a go-between concerning our divorce.

Yeah, I'm divorcing him. I've seen an attorney to file for divorce. It's over for us, and I'm ready to close the book on that chapter in my life.

I talk to Christian about once a week. He calls to check up on me. I kid him that old habits are hard to kick. He always laughs at that, which is something he doesn't do a lot of lately. He is hurting so badly. Sometimes I feel so close and so at peace talking to him because I feel like we have survived a war together. Yet other times it is so emotionally draining to talk to him because Christian always reminds me of *him*. There is no way, at this point, that I can separate the two in my mind. But I think, no I know, Christian will remain in my life in some form or fashion because he is definitely a "keeper," as Mama would say.

Oh, I've found a job. I found one once I stopped feeling sorry for myself and got up out of bed. I have realized my dream to become an elementary-school teacher. I can honestly say that I love my job. My "children" are an adorable bunch of third graders. They are the ones who have kept me sane and gotten me through this ordeal. They are my joy. There's this one little girl, Briana, who is always telling me that she wants to grow up and be a teacher just like me!

I can feel myself getting stronger and stronger each day. I'm learning to love myself again. I'll just have to take it one step at a time, like a recovering alcoholic. I think I can do it. In fact, I know I can do it. I have learned my lessons in love and learned them well.

Electa Rome Parks currently lives outside Atlanta, Georgia, with her husband, Nelson, and their two children. With a BA degree in marketing, she is presently working on her next novel and fulfilling her passion as a writer.

The Ties That Bind

Electa Rome Parks

A CONVERSATION WITH
ELECTA ROME PARKS

Q. What can you tell your readers about Electa Rome Parks?

A. Umm, that's a hard question. It's not easy to define or describe oneself in a condensed version, but I'll try. I was born and raised in Georgia. So yes, I'm a true Georgia peach, even though I lived in Chicago and North Carolina for many years. Basically, I'm just your average, down-to-earth wife and mother of two who has a great passion for writing and reading. Honestly, I don't think I could live without books and the written word. I've found that a pen to paper is a powerful tool!

Let's see, what else can I divulge about myself and keep you interested? (Smile) Believe it or not, I'm actually kinda quiet and laid-back. I can be moody and oversensitive (Pisces trait). So . . . be careful what you say about *The Ties That Bind,* because I'm sensitive about my stuff (LOL).

I have a very vivid imagination, which is evident in my books, and I believe in a lot of theories that most people would think bizarre. Let's just say I absolutely love *X-Files* and the entire concept of spirits, guardian angels and karma. I once had a palm reader tell me I was a writer in another life and that's why writing validates and elevates me to be in complete sync with my spirit. I thought that was so deep and so unbelievably true.

Bottom line, anyone who truly knows me will state that I'm real. I'm very approachable and I have a genuine caring nature (another Pisces trait). I have my "few" imperfections and struggles just like the next person. However, I believe in order to really get in touch with our true spirit, we need to discover our gifts. I feel that we are all born into the world with a special gift, and I've found mine. That brings me great joy!

What else? I pretty much suck at any sport, my favorite color is purple, I've never weighed more than 112 pounds my entire life, my all-time favorite movie is a toss between *Soul Food* and *The Best Man* and I have tons of stories to share with my readers.

Q. Who has been your writing inspiration?

A. I have a great love and admiration for contemporary writers such as Terry McMillan, Eric Jerome Dickey, Bebe Moore Campbell, E. Lynn Harris, Kimberla Lawson Roby, to name a few. For me, reading and writing go hand in hand. I read for entertainment, to relax and unwind, to take a minivacation for 250 pages or so. Through reading I travel to new places and meet new and interesting people without ever leaving the comfort of my home. Amazing. So I tend to write that way. I like for my readers to feel as though I'm letting them in on some juicy gossip and that my characters are talking directly to them. I'm a very emotional person, and my characters tend to be, as well.

Additionally, contemporary writers were the first ones to inspire me to follow my dreams. I vividly remember the first time I read *Disappearing Acts* by Terry McMillan. I was in absolute, undeniable awe. I discovered characters that looked like me, talked like me, acted like me, and I savored each and every word like a fine gourmet dinner. I felt the characters' pain, triumphs and joy because I could relate. I didn't want that novel to end. It was with true sadness that I read the last page. From that point forward, it was on; I devoured any African-American fiction I could get my hands on; I was addicted. To this day, I'm still addicted.

If I want to be real deep and philosophical for a few days, I read Toni Morrison, Alice Walker or Gloria Naylor. They always elevate my spirit and mind to a higher plane. Their words soothe my soul with their wisdom and insight. I've enjoyed the classics as well with such writers as Zora Neale Hurston, Ralph Ellison and James Baldwin.

Additionally, I adore Stephen King and Dean Koontz because I'm a big supernatural/horror fan.

Q. Describe your writing style.

A. (LOL) There is no name or definition to define my writing style; it's pretty unorthodox. To put it simply, I go with the flow. I come up with a general storyline in my head, and then I simply sit down in front of my PC and start typing. I don't believe in outlines, or at least, I can't function in a writing environment with one.

When I'm writing, I have no idea what my beginning, middle or ending is. However, I know my characters like the back of my hand. I could tell you what they got for their twelfth birthday down to what they ate for lunch two weeks ago. In writing, I let my characters talk to me and dictate their story. Sometimes we fight about how a certain scene should play out, but in the long run, they win. Yes, it's weird, but true.

Q. What type of atmosphere do you require to write?

A. When I really get into a writing project, it doesn't matter what type of atmosphere I surround myself with. The words will flow naturally.

A lot of times, I mentally write my chapters when I'm driving. I can drive, zone out mentally (without causing an accident) and come up with great dialogue and an additional chapter or two. When I arrive home, I swiftly run to my PC and simply type it before I forget. So it's like I'm writing down what I saw at a movie or play with great detail included.

If I had to name a preference, I prefer a somewhat quiet, relaxing, peaceful atmosphere.

Q. What has been the most gratifying part of being an author?

A. Hands down, the most gratifying part of being an author has been meeting and greeting new and interesting readers who embrace my stories and e-mail me and write me and meet me at signings and tell me how much they've enjoyed my books! We talk about my characters like they are old friends. No matter how many times I've experienced that, it always makes my day. Puts a big Kool-Aid smile on my face (LOL).

Their (the readers) feedback and reactions totally validate that my craft is a gift from God! If I can touch a number of people with my stories, or even if I only entertain them and they don't walk away with a life lesson, then I've still done my job.

As you know, my stories are typically relationship based, very drama filled with an ounce of spice thrown in—well maybe a pound of spice thrown in—and they usually cover a topical issue that is prevalent in today's society. Believe me, I have so many characters screaming inside my head, waiting to tell their story, that I feel like the lady from the movie *Sybil* (LOL). So, bottom line, I pray and claim that my readership base will continue to grow and I'll have wonderful opportunities to meet many more fans.

Q. *What inspired you to write* The Ties That Bind?

A. *The Ties That Bind* is just one of the stories that I carried around in my head for many years. Whenever I had a quiet moment, I'd mentally add on another chapter. Mia was always my primary character because she reminded me of so many women who are looking for their Mr. Right. I asked myself some "what if" questions such as, "What if Mia meets a man who she *thinks* is the one, only to find out once she has gotten caught up in the relationship that he has a lot of issues he needs to address?"

Once Mia, Brice and Christian started showing up in my dreams, I felt it was time to put them on paper.

Q. *Why did you choose to write about spousal abuse?*

A. I'm an avid reader, period, but I particularly enjoy relationship stories, and that's probably why I prefer to write in that genre. However, for *The Ties That Bind,* I wanted a relationship story, but I also wanted to deal with some topical issues as well. I wanted to write about an issue that was very real and prevalent in today's relationships. I wanted to write about a topic that may be pushed under the carpet because no one wants to get involved in family matters or matters of the heart. Spousal abuse came to the forefront.

Q. What messages would you like readers to receive from reading The Ties That Bind?

A. I'm a realist and I know that in real life, relationships do not always have a happily ever after ending. That seems to be a central theme in many relationship stories. In the end, the girl gets the boy, then they skip off, hand in hand, into oblivion and they live happily ever after. Not! That's not always life. That's Harlequin romance novels. (I hear some amens in the corner over there.)

I wanted to write realistically about the flip side of relationships where there may be some topical issues going on larger than *him* cheating on *her* or vice versa.

Mia represented a collage of women I've met during my lifetime who are looking for their soul mates in life. Unfortunately, a lot of times, they are looking for someone to make them happy and complete them, and they haven't quite figured out you have to be happy with yourself first. Love yourself first and then you won't be willing to put up with a lot of BS. In fact, you won't allow yourself to be treated as anything less than a Nubian queen.

Q. How can readers get in contact with you?

A. My readers can keep abreast of my writing career through my Web site at www.electaromeparks.com. And please, readers, drop me a line, give me some feedback (remember I'm sensitive, now), just holla at a sista at novelideal@aol.com.

QUESTIONS FOR DISCUSSION

1. Do you believe that two people can date for a short period of time (thirty days) and fall in love? Is it possible to truly know someone and feel close to someone in such a short time frame?

2. Was Mia's decision to marry Brice based on love or an attempt to escape an alcoholic mother? Was Mia too young and immature to marry Brice? Could Mia have ever been the type of wife Brice was looking for?

3. After Brice hit Mia the first time, should she have left him? Is it true, if he hits you once, he will hit you again? Were there earlier indications that Brice was capable of hitting Mia?

4. Did Brice love Mia in his own way? Do you feel that Brice's upbringing, seeing his mother physically abused by his father, contributed to his own behavior? Did Brice feel his behavior towards Mia was justified?

5. What do you think of the age difference of eight years between Mia and Brice? Was Brice too old/mature/worldly for Mia? Was Mia looking for a father figure in Brice?

6. Can a man like Brice change his ways/behavior? At the end of the story, was Brice sorry for "the incident" or was he sorry that Mia left him? Were you surprised that Mia left Brice?

7. Was Christian a true friend/brother to Brice? Should Christian have intervened once he found out about the spousal abuse going on in Brice and Mia's marriage?

8. What would you do if you were in a similar situation? Would you intervene or stay out of the situation? Is physical abuse still a taboo subject?

9. Was Christian in love with Mia or just infatuated? Should he have confessed his true feelings to Mia? To Brice?

10. If Christian hadn't knocked on Mia's door, what do you feel would have happened between Mia and Malcolm? Was Mia wrong in her actions or pushed into the situation with Malcolm because of her desire to be loved?

11. What ties bound the main characters to each other? By the end of the story, were these ties forever severed?

12. It's five years later: Where do you see Mia, Brice and Christian at in their lives?